"I don't think dinner's a good idea."

"Why ever not?"

Sally looked up then, and her blue eyes shone with an unnatural intensity. "It would be too much like a date."

"And that's a crime?"

"You're my boss, remember?"

"Well, yes. That's…true." Logan scratched his jaw. Somehow, his original plan to keep business and pleasure apart no longer made any sense. He was quite sure that he and Sally should have dinner together. The sooner the better. "Let's keep work out of this. You'll be sacrificing your evenings to help me. Surely I owe you one dinner?"

From city girl—to corporate wife!

They're working side by side, nine to five....
But no matter how hard these couples
try to keep their relationships strictly professional,
romance is undeniably on the agenda!

But will a date in the office diary lead to an
appointment at the altar?

Find out in this exciting miniseries.

If you love office-romance stories, look out for

In January 2009
Promoted: Secretary to Bride!
by Jennie Adams

With a new dress and a borrowed pair of hopes-and-dreams shoes on her feet, mousy Molly is transformed for a posh work party, but will it be enough to catch the eye of her brooding boss, Jarrod?

In February 2009
Manhattan Boss, Diamond Proposal
by Trish Wylie

She's made it to Manhattan, but can girl-next-door Clare capture the heart of her playboy boss, Quinn, and make it down the aisle?

BARBARA HANNAY

Blind Date with the Boss

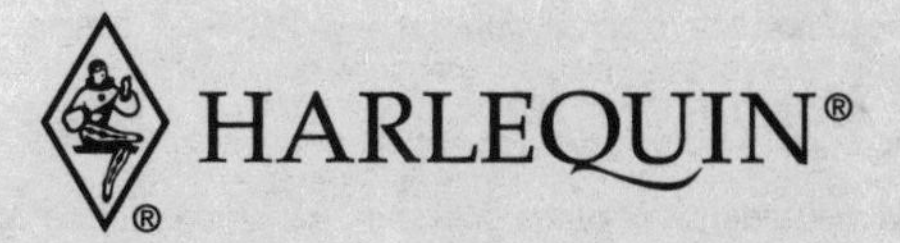

TORONTO • NEW YORK • LONDON
AMSTERDAM • PARIS • SYDNEY • HAMBURG
STOCKHOLM • ATHENS • TOKYO • MILAN • MADRID
PRAGUE • WARSAW • BUDAPEST • AUCKLAND

ISBN-13: 978-0-373-17550-5
ISBN-10: 0-373-17550-7

BLIND DATE WITH THE BOSS

First North American Publication 2008.

This edition published by arrangement with Harlequin Books S.A.

www.eHarlequin.com

Printed in U.S.A.

Barbara Hannay was born in Sydney, educated in Brisbane, and has spent most of her adult life living in tropical North Queensland, where she and her husband have raised four children. While she has enjoyed many happy times camping and canoeing in the bush, she also delights in an urban lifestyle—chamber music, contemporary dance, movies and dining out. An English teacher, she has always loved writing, and now, by having her stories published, she is living her most cherished fantasy.

Visit www.barbarahannay.com.

Make a date in your diary
for Barbara Hannay's next book:
HER CATTLEMAN BOSS
On sale March next year.

With special thanks to Victoria, my daughter,
who knows how to dance.

CHAPTER ONE

SALLY FINCH stood before the mirror in the pretty terrace house she had recently inherited and knew she'd made a huge mistake.

So much depended on today's job interview. If she didn't start earning soon, she wouldn't be able to stay in this gorgeous old house that she'd loved since she was six years old. She couldn't start her new life as an independent woman in the city. Bottom line, she couldn't eat!

But as Sally studied the results of this morning's careful grooming, she was swamped by doubts—niggling at first, but growing stronger with every twist and turn in front of the mirror.

Until this moment, she'd been confident that she knew exactly how to dress for a big city interview, but the mirror posed an uncomfortable question. Shouldn't she, at the very least, be able to recognise her own reflection?

What had gone wrong?

She'd woken early in a fever of confident excitement, had sung in the shower, eaten a super-healthy breakfast of fresh fruit and yoghurt in Chloe's cheerful, sun-filled kitchen—she still thought of this house as her godmother's—and then she'd raced upstairs to her bedroom.

The new and too expensive navy-blue dress fitted like a dream. Made from fine merino wool, with a high neckline and a neat white collar, it fell in straight, slim lines to a softly flared hemline. Its simplicity and neatness, Sally fervently hoped, signalled the very essence of efficiency.

Intent on completing her efficient image, she'd carefully brushed and crammed every wayward wisp of her blonde curling hair under hairpins and into a tight knot at the back of her head.

And then she'd stepped back to appraise the results and saw, with a chilling certainty, that she looked as grim and forbidding as her unforgettable third grade teacher.

How had this happened? The neck to knee navy had looked flattering in the shop. 'Fabulous' was the word the shop assistant had used.

Now the dress made Sally look too thin.

Admittedly, she had always been on the light side. Her older brothers had teased her about it when she was a skinny kid and she hadn't given two hoots. Dressed in their hand-me-down jeans, sensible cotton shirts and sturdy riding boots, she'd simply been one of the gang, riding horses or quad bikes all over her family's Outback property at Tarra-Binya.

Today, however, at the age of twenty-three and on the brink of life as a city woman, Sally would have loved to show more of her womanly curves.

She wondered what Chloe would have thought of this outfit. Her godmother had had a brilliant sense of style, and an even greater capacity for living life to the full. She'd been sensitive and warm-hearted too and had always said exactly the right thing to make Sally feel good about herself.

That she wasn't here to help Sally phase into city life was almost too much to bear.

Blinking back tears she couldn't afford on such an important morning, Sally tipped her head from side to side and swiftly switched her attention to her hair. Perhaps that was an even bigger problem than the dress. She'd overdone the efficient image.

After all, her interview at Blackcorp Mining Consultancies was for a front desk job and, if she got it, she would be meeting people all day long. And, although the Human Resources manager at Blackcorp would require efficiency in a receptionist, she would be expecting friendliness too.

Friendliness was Sally's forte. She loved people and loved to chat, had always hoped for a job that involved plenty of talking. But now, as she practised smiling into the mirror, forced a sparkle into her eyes and gave a cheerful flash of her white teeth, she still looked like the Wicked Witch of the West.

That hair knot has to go.

Frantically, she began to rip out hairpins. She didn't really have time to start rearranging her appearance, but she couldn't face her appointment looking like this.

Pins scattered left and right, hitting the glass tray, the polished timber dressing table, the carpeted floor. Sally paid little heed to them as blonde curls bobbed up, like coiled springs, happy to be free again.

The front doorbell rang.

No.

Not now! Who on earth would be calling at eight o'clock on a Monday morning? She was only halfway through the rescue attempt on her hair.

Unwilling to waste precious time by going all the way downstairs to the door, Sally dashed to the bedroom window, conveniently poised above the front steps. With a flick of the curtain, she could identify her caller.

'Anna!'

Her sister-in-law was almost jogging on the top step, balancing her young daughter, Rose, on her hip while she pressed the doorbell again.

'I'm up here,' Sally called.

Anna Finch looked up, her face chalk-white and terrified. Sally's first thought was that something had happened to Steve, her brother, who worked on an oil rig off the Western Australian coast.

Without another word, she left the window and flew down the stairs, her hair problems instantly dismissed.

'Anna,' she cried as she flung the front door open and encountered a heart-stopping close up view of her sister-in-law's pale cheeks and fearful, worried eyes. 'What is it? What's the matter? Is it Steve?'

'No, Steve's fine. It's Oliver. He's having a terrible asthma attack.'

It was only then that Sally saw Anna's blue car parked at the gate and her three-year-old nephew's sad face peering anxiously out at them. Poor little Oliver looked pale and sunken and, even from this distance, Sally could sense that he was struggling to breathe.

'I rang the doctor's surgery and they told me to take him straight to the hospital,' Anna said.

'The poor darling. How can I help?'

'I was hoping you could mind Rose.' As she said this, Anna thrust her chubby young daughter into Sally's arms. 'Oliver's so frightened and I'm almost as terrified as he is.'

Sally could believe that. Anna was often in a state of high anxiety, one of those mothers who were perpetually worried. And this time she had a real emergency on her hands.

'I don't think I could manage at the hospital if I had Rose with me as well,' she said.

Sally nearly said, *I have my interview this morning*, but she bit it back. Anna had enough on her plate.

'I knew you wouldn't mind.' Without checking Sally's response, Anna slipped the strap of a large crimson vinyl bag from her shoulder and set it on the doorstep. 'Everything Rose needs should be in here.'

'Right.' Sally looked at the fifteen-month-old toddler in her arms—all golden hair and sunshiny smiles—and her heart sank. What on earth could she do with Rose while she went to the interview? She was already in danger of running late. And her hopes were pinned on scoring this job. Already, an alarming number of bills had landed in her letter box.

'You're wonderful, Sal,' Anna said. 'It's so great having you close by now.' At the bottom of the steps, she seemed to remember something. 'What on earth have you done to your hair?'

'Oh.' Sally knew she must look a fright with one half of her hair still in pins. She shrugged and a hysterical little laugh escaped her. 'It's—it's an experiment. I was trying a new look.'

With an unflattering roll of her eyes and a shake of her head, Anna raced back to her car.

Logan Black sat in his office, which was perched like an eagle's eyrie high above Sydney's glittering blue harbour, and spoke smoothly into the phone. 'I'm sorry to disappoint you, Charles, but I couldn't consider that proposal without—'

Logan stopped in mid-sentence. He wasn't easily distracted from a business conversation, but he could have sworn he'd heard a giggle coming from beneath his desk.

But that was impossible.

Ridiculous.

'As I was saying, I—' He paused again. This time he'd felt a distinct tug on the lace of his right shoe.

What the devil?

Swivelling in his leather executive chair, he peered into the shadowy depths beneath his enormous cherry wood desk and almost dropped the phone.

A very small child grinned cheekily up at him—a little girl, if Logan guessed correctly—not much more than a baby really. Her face was distinctly impish and she was clutching Logan's shoelace in her tiny pink fist.

Logan cursed and then blustered, 'How did you get in here?'

'What's that? What are you talking about?' The CEO of Australia's biggest mining company was suddenly confused and impatient on the other end of the line.

'Ah—one moment, Charles.' Logan stared down at the tiny intruder. How had a baby materialised in his office? In *his* office—the inner sanctum of the Managing Director of Blackcorp Mining Consultancies? It didn't make sense. The occasional attractive woman might have found her way in here unannounced, but that was another matter entirely.

Surely it was impossible for any trespasser to enter here without being seen. Had the child crawled? Or was she simply so small she'd been out of eye range? Below the radar, so to speak.

With his hand over the receiver, Logan pressed the button connecting him to his PA's desk and, at the same time, he barked, 'Maria!'

To his dismay, there was no reply from outside and no reassuring female figure appeared at the doorway. To make matters worse, the little trespasser had abandoned Logan's shoelaces and seemed intent on climbing his leg, clasping at the fine wool of his expensive trousers with distinctly sticky paws.

'Down!' Logan ordered in much the same voice he might have used to scold a wilful puppy.

'Logan, what the hell's going on?' Charles Holmes's voice thundered into the phone.

'I'm sorry, Charles.' Eyeing the toddler with an emotion approaching horror, Logan cleared his throat. Where was Maria? 'Something's—er—come up. An emergency. I'll have to call you back. I'll email through my suggestions for the changes and then we'll take another look at your proposal.'

As he hung up, Logan scowled at the small person now trying to straddle his knee. Her eyes were dark brown and enormous, like a puppy's, her hair super-fine and shiny gold, her skin soft and pink.

She looked deceptively angelic, smelled of shampoo and was dressed neatly in a pink dress embroidered with ducks. Her shoes were soft leather, her socks clean and white. She had, Logan admitted silently, the noticeable attributes of a child whose mother cared for her. This morning, however, her mother had been noticeably care*less*.

'Where are your parents?' Logan demanded aloud.

'Jig-jig!' the baby girl replied, bouncing vigorously on his Italian-shod foot.

'No, I will not jig-jig.' Gingerly fitting his hands beneath her tiny armpits, Logan lifted her before she could scramble any higher and set her back on the floor. 'I don't have time to jig-jig. I have a company to run. We need to find your parents.'

Again he pressed the buzzer on his desk and, when there was no answer, he marched to his office doorway and glared at the abandoned PA's desk. If Maria was engaged elsewhere, he would have to call the front desk. Surely someone knew where this child belonged.

Behind him, Logan heard another disturbing giggle.

The little girl was under the desk again, peeking out at him and grinning mischievously, as if they'd begun a new game of hide and seek.

For a moment Logan felt an unexpected warm sensation in his chest. The baby was undeniably cute and he thought of his nephews, his sister's boys. He really should visit Carissa more often.

But he was snapped right out of this uncharacteristic

moment of sentiment when a chubby pink hand reached for the dangling cord attached to his computer.

'No, kid. No!'

Five years ago Logan had been proud of his rugby tackles, but today, as he hurled himself into a low dive across the office carpet, he knew he was already too slow and too late.

CHAPTER TWO

THE interview was going rather well, Sally thought. She'd made it in the nick of time, her curls restored to their usual disorganized bounciness, and Janet Keaton, Blackcorp's HR manager, had been incredibly understanding when she'd telephoned to explain about her last-minute babysitting emergency.

'I really need to complete the interviews today,' Janet had said. 'Perhaps you'd better bring your niece with you. Do you think she would sit in the corner of my office while we talk?'

'I can't promise she'll be quiet,' Sally had warned. 'But I'll bring a bag of her toys and her favourite picture books.'

Janet's voice had been reassuringly warm. 'Let's give it a try. I might not be able to reschedule your time slot.'

Fortunately, a rescheduling hadn't been necessary. Rose, bless her, had become completely absorbed in pushing brightly coloured shapes through holes in a plastic box and then opening the box to take the shapes out, before starting the process all over again. And Sally had become equally absorbed in Janet Keaton's interesting questions.

She was quizzed about her childhood at Tarra-Binya, about her boarding school days in a big country town and the computer course she'd completed on leaving school. She'd told

Janet about her summer holiday jobs on the front desk of Chloe's art gallery here in Sydney at Potts Point. And that led to Sally explaining about her godmother, Chloe Porter, a well-known figure in Sydney's art circles, and about her legacy of the terrace house.

'And you didn't mind leaving the country to live in Sydney?' Janet asked.

Sally almost blurted the truth that she'd had to leave, that she'd had to escape her family's stifling concern, had to prove that she could manage on her own. But she doubted that would impress her interviewer.

'I've always wanted to live here,' she said emphatically, and this was also very true. 'It's been my dream. I spent nearly every summer holiday with Chloe and it was always so much fun. I love Sydney. It's so cosmopolitan and exciting. I'm really looking forward to making my home here.'

'A mining consultancy is very different from an art gallery,' Janet said carefully. 'What do you know about Blackcorp and the Australian mining industry?'

'Well…' Sally took a deep breath and thanked heavens that she'd looked at Blackcorp's website on the Internet. 'I know that Blackcorp's a big operation right across Australia. Mining's a huge industry and it's bigger than ever right now. Actually, two of my brothers work in mines. One in Queensland and another in Western Australia.'

Janet nodded and waited for Sally to continue.

'China's Australia's major market,' she said. 'And I guess a consultancy like this would be offering support services—accommodation on the mine sites, catering. And there are all kinds of environmental issues to be worked around.'

By then Sally had exhausted her knowledge and she thought she might have flunked, but Janet smiled encouragingly and gave her a questionnaire to answer.

'This simply provides a profile of your personality type. There are no right or wrong answers. It will be useful if you join our staff and become involved in the team-building exercises I like to run.'

Team-building exercises definitely sounded like Sally's cup of tea. She had loved that sort of thing at school.

'Just choose the response that feels natural to you,' Janet said.

Already smiling, Sally glanced at the first few questions on the quiz sheet.

You find it difficult to be the centre of attention. Yes? No?

You trust reason rather than emotions. Yes? No?

You rarely get excited. Yes? No?

'Oh, goodness!' Janet's sharp cry interrupted Sally's concentration. 'Where's the little girl?'

One hasty glance at the abandoned toys in the corner and Sally's stomach plummeted. The office door was ominously ajar and a quick look around the room revealed that Rose had disappeared.

Launched to her feet, she hurried outside with Janet close behind. The carpeted corridor was empty.

'I'm so sorry,' Sally said, feeling sick. 'Rose has been so good. I forgot to keep my eye on her.'

Janet shook her head. 'She can't be far away. She couldn't have got into the lift by herself, so she must still be somewhere on this floor. You try the offices on the right-hand side and I'll take the left.'

'Thank you.' Sally realised she was shaking. How could she have forgotten about Rose? Poor Anna had trusted her. She shouldn't have been so caught up with wanting this job. What kind of aunt *lost* her niece on the twenty-seventh floor of a skyscraper?

The first door on her right bore the brass-lettered sign: *Accounts*. Sally swallowed a knot of fear and stepped forward but, as she lifted her hand to knock, she saw, out of the corner of her eye, a tall dark shape at the end of the corridor.

She caught a flash of golden hair and she whirled about. Rose. In the arms of a man.

Oh, gosh. Not just any man.

This one looked formidable. One glance and Sally's impulse to run forward, arms outstretched, a grateful smile on her lips, was stifled. Big-shouldered, long-legged, dark and frowning, he came towards her, striding down the corridor with Rose at arm's length in front of him, as if the poor darling were a bag of extremely unpleasant garbage.

Janet, who had seen him too, let out a groan and Sally received the distinct impression that Rose couldn't have chosen a more unsuitable saviour.

As the frowning man approached, Sally noticed details beyond his scowl and his athletic physique. He was undeniably handsome, but there was a steely edge to his looks that sent unwelcome shivers scampering through her. His hair was thick and dark and already, before noon, there were signs of a five o'clock shadow on his jaw. His eyes were dark too, and penetrating, even at twenty paces.

Memories threatened, but Sally forced them back. She was no longer afraid of every new man she met. Those days were behind her.

She smiled at this man in his expensively cut dark suit, crisp white business shirt and smart navy and silver striped tie. He had the air of a commander. Executive material, Sally supposed.

By comparison, Rose looked tiny and fragile. But so-o cute. And, thank heavens, completely unharmed.

The darling. Sally held out her arms and Rose was thrust immediately into her embrace. If she hadn't had so much experience in receiving her brothers' football passes, she might have dropped the poor child.

'Thank you.' She offered the frowning figure her warmest smile. 'Thank you so much. I'm so grateful you found her. We were just about to start a search party.'

'Was Rose in your office, Logan?' Janet asked. 'I can't believe she got so far.'

'I found her under my desk.' He spoke without the faintest glimmer of warmth. 'What on earth's going on, Janet? You haven't started a crèche here, have you?'

'Oh, that's my fault,' Sally butted in quickly, anxious that Janet Keaton shouldn't take any blame. 'There was a family emergency at the last minute and I had to bring Rose with me,' she said. 'I'm sorry if she interrupted you.'

Janet added diplomatically, 'At least Rose is too little to have done any harm.'

'She disconnected my computer.'

'Oh, Rose,' Sally scolded softly.

To Janet he said, 'I'll need someone from IT up here straight away. I've lost an entire morning's work.'

Now it was Sally's turn to frown. 'Surely you'd already saved most of it?'

'Sally,' Janet intervened in a strange little voice, 'let me introduce Blackcorp's Managing Director, Mr Logan Black.'

'Oh.'

Managing Director. I've been acting the smart mouth with the head honcho. Good one, Sally.

Her confident smile slipped as she held out her hand. 'Pleased to meet you, Mr Black.'

'This is Sally Finch, Logan. She's one of our applicants for the front desk position.'

At least Logan Black was polite enough to shake Sally's proffered hand firmly, but his right eyebrow lifted and he eyed her with faint contempt.

She might have told Mr Black how very keen she was to work for his company, but her recent gaffe and the curl of his lip, *plus* Janet Keaton's warning frown, ensured that she remained prudently quiet.

Rose chose that moment to grumble and rub at her eyes. It was getting close to her nap time. Sally rocked her gently and kissed the top of her head and Rose pressed her sleepy head against Sally's breast.

Logan Black stared at them and his stern frown faded. Sally saw a softening in his expression, a fleeting hint of a different emotion that made her wonder if he was as tough as he made out.

But the moment was over quickly and, almost immediately, he gave a curt nod, turned abruptly and marched back down the corridor.

'Well…' Janet Keaton glanced at her wristwatch. 'I'm afraid we've run out of time, Sally.'

'But I didn't finish your personality test.'

'Don't worry. You can always fill that in later. If you get the job.'

If you get the job…

Sally felt flat as she collected Rose's things and bade Janet farewell.

'We should make our decision within the next few days,' Janet said and she smiled, but Sally didn't find this very reassuring.

She'd always had good antennae, could pick up vibes very quickly, and she'd been sure that everything about the interview had been going swimmingly until Logan Black had arrived with Rose. Then, between them, the man and the baby had destroyed every ion of positive atmosphere.

Late in the afternoon, Logan Black ducked his head around Janet Keaton's office doorway. She was working at her desk when she heard his knock, but she looked up and smiled.

He frowned at her. 'Have you finished your interviews for that front desk position?'

'All done.'

'I assume the other applicants were less encumbered than the cheeky single mother I met this morning.'

Janet narrowed her eyes at Logan. 'There were no cheeky single mothers among the people I interviewed.'

'You know who I mean. The blonde with the runaway daughter.'

'Sally Finch?'

Logan nodded. He was terrible with names, but yes, hers had been something to do with a bird.

'I think Sally's confident rather than cheeky. Anyway, she isn't the little girl's mother.'

'She isn't?'

'No.' Janet looked as if she was about to expand on this, but suddenly she folded her arms and leaned forward with her elbows resting on her desk. A thoughtful frown creased her brow. 'Why the sudden interrogation, Logan? This isn't like you.'

'What do you mean? It's in my interests to vet my company's employees.' His hand strayed to scratch the back of his neck.

'But I've been your HR manager for almost four years and you've never interfered. You've always trusted my judgement.'

This, Logan knew, was very true. Janet had always consulted him about positions in management, but he'd let her have free rein with the recruitment of lower echelon staff and he'd always been happy with her choices.

'I don't think we should be too hard on Sally,' Janet went on. 'There was a medical emergency and she was doing someone in her family a good turn.'

Logan's jaw set stubbornly. He wished he'd never started this silly conversation.

It was bad enough that all day he'd kept remembering the girl with her mass of blonde curls. Despite the unflattering fluorescent office lighting, her hair had shone like spun gold and he'd found himself thinking, ridiculously, that it must look incredibly pretty in sunlight. Worse, he kept seeing her with the child in her arms, couldn't forget the sight of her dipping her head to comfort the little girl with a soft kiss.

What was the matter with him? She wasn't his type at all, and he truly didn't give two hoots if she got the job or not.

'You're quite right,' he told Janet. 'I'll leave the selection of a receptionist in your capable hands.'

'Thank you, Logan,' Janet said dryly. As he turned to leave, she added, 'But, while you're here, can you take one of these personality tests to fill in? It's part of my preparation for the next team-building workshop.'

'Team-building? But that won't involve me. I don't have the time right now.'

Janet rose majestically and shook the stapled sheets of paper at him. 'You promised your full support.'

'But I didn't… That doesn't mean…'

'It means you've signed up for the Blackcorp team-building workshop, Logan. You promised top down involvement in this one.'

Next morning the phone never seemed to stop ringing. Each time Sally heard its shrill summons, she thought it might be a call from Blackcorp and her stomach tied itself in anxious knots.

She tried to distract herself by entertaining Rose, who had stayed with her overnight while Anna slept on a folding bed at the hospital.

Warm sunlight filled the little paved courtyard that opened off the kitchen, so she took Rose out there and gave her a large cardboard carton to play with. Growing up in the Outback had taught her that the simplest playthings were often the best.

The baby had a delightful time crawling into the cardboard box and out again, then piling her teddy bear and stuffed rabbit into it and, of course, hauling them out once more.

Watching her, Sally gave a rueful shake of her head. 'Why are you being so well behaved today, after what you did to me yesterday?'

Rose simply grinned and gurgled.

While the baby played, Sally went through the newspapers from the weekend, circling more jobs that she could apply for. Then she attacked the little garden that bordered the courtyard, pulling weeds and trimming overgrown shrubs, tying trailing vines of white star jasmine to a timber lattice.

Every time the phone rang, she had to dash, heart thumping, in through the open French windows to the kitchen, peeling off gardening gloves as she ran.

The first call was from Anna with an overnight report on Oliver, who was much better. Sally reassured her sister-in-law that Rose was fine and invited her to lunch, suggesting that she needed a break from the hospital and Anna accepted readily.

Two people phoned asking to speak to Chloe and Sally had to pass on the sad news of Chloe's heart attack. Then there was a call from Sally's mother, ringing long distance from Tarra-Binya to check that Sally was eating properly and not just buying those terrible take-aways that were on every street corner in the city.

Sally, who by this time had made a lovely Salade Niçoise for Anna's lunch, assured her mother that she was not in danger of malnutrition just yet. But, as she replaced the receiver, she thought that she might be starving soon if she didn't land a job.

Whenever she thought about yesterday's interview, she cringed. In the cold light of another day, it was patently clear that she'd been too smart-mouthed. She'd been so determined that Logan Black mustn't intimidate her, had needed to prove to herself that she was no longer afraid of hot-looking guys who were way too sexy for their T-shirts.

But she'd gone too far and she'd annoyed her potential boss and she'd shocked Janet Keaton. She should have remembered how vitally important it was to make a good first impression.

The problem was, she *really* wanted that job. She wanted, more than anything, to prove to her family that she was fine now, that she could stand on her own two feet and, in order to do that, she needed money. But her reasons for wanting the job went deeper than that, and they had nothing to do with a certain tall, dark and sternly handsome boss.

She'd seen Blackcorp's sleek, modern front desk standing just inside the big glass sliding front doors and she'd visualised herself there, accepting important packages from the delivery man, relaying mail or visitors to various departments, getting to know all the employees and greeting them as they arrived at work each day.

She wanted that position so badly she couldn't bring herself to follow up on any of the other advertisements she'd found. And that was silly. This afternoon, just as soon as she handed Rose back to Anna, she would have to resume her job-hunting in earnest.

Sally was enjoying lunch out in the courtyard with Anna and Rose when the phone rang again.

Her stomach tied itself into yet another knot as she darted inside and she was a little puffed when she picked up the phone. 'Hello? Sally speaking.'

'Hi, Sally. It's Janet Keaton from Blackcorp.'

A blast of heat exploded in Sally's chest, like a small bomb, sending flashes over her arms and up her neck.

'Janet,' she squeaked. Good grief, what was the matter with her? She'd never felt this nervous about *anything*. 'How—how are you?'

'Very well, thank you, Sally. And I have some good news.'

'Y-you do?'

'I'd like to offer you our front desk position.'

Normally quite good at filling awkward silences, Sally was suddenly too shaken and surprised to utter a single syllable.

'I assume you're still interested?' Janet eventually enquired.

'Oh, yes,' Sally managed at last. 'I'm very interested. It's fantastic news. I'm thrilled.'

Stunned would be a better word, but somehow she was able to listen carefully while Janet explained about her starting salary and details like superannuation and staff induction. She returned to the lunch table in a daze.

'Have you had bad news?' Anna asked.

'No, on the contrary.' Sally gave a shaky laugh. 'I've got a job.'

'Really? That's wonderful. I hadn't even realised you'd applied for one.'

Sally grinned. 'It's with Blackcorp.'

'Blackcorp? Wow! They're from the big end of town. When did all this happen?'

'I had the interview yesterday.'

Anna's eyes widened. 'But you were minding Rose yesterday.'

'I know.' Sally suppressed a strange urge to giggle. 'Amazing, isn't it? They couldn't change my appointment, so they let me take Rose with me. I hope you don't mind.'

'Of course I don't mind. I trust you to look after my little sweetheart.' Anna gave her daughter a proud motherly pat. 'She must have been very well behaved.'

'She was…quiet as a mouse,' Sally assured her truthfully.

CHAPTER THREE

SALLY started work at Blackcorp on the following Monday morning and by lunch time she knew she was going to love it. Most of the employees were very friendly and many of them stopped at her desk to say hello and to introduce themselves before continuing on through the security doors.

The switchboard was modern, simple and efficient to operate, with a computer list of staff that was easy to access and connect. After the first few calls, Sally began to feel some of the initial stress leave her.

Logan Black strode in, briefcase in one hand, mobile phone in the other, all clean-cut and drop-dead handsome. He almost ignored her, but then he turned abruptly and stared at her with a puzzled frown. Sally wished her throat didn't feel so dry.

For rather longer than was necessary, her boss's gaze settled on her. To Sally's surprise, his frown melted and an unguarded light flared in his eyes, the beginnings of warmth and the promise of a smile—an exceptionally gorgeous smile, she suspected. She feared her legs might give way.

But the reckless moment was over in a flash and Logan Black quickly recovered. His frown returned, he gave her a curt nod and said, 'Morning, Miss Sparrow.' And he kept walking.

Miss Sparrow?

Sally opened her mouth to remind her employer, ever so politely, that her name was *Finch*. But she remembered her new resolution to be more circumspect, so she swallowed her pride, lifted her chin and smiled warmly as she offered a cheery, 'Good morning, Mr Black.'

He'd already passed her and she was speaking to his back.

How annoying to feel so flustered by the brief encounter. *Get control, girl. You'll be seeing him every day.*

Her work kept her busy and there was no chance to be bored. There seemed to be an endless stream of deliveries. All shapes and sizes of boxes were wheeled in on trolleys and important-looking express courier packets arrived, as well as bags of mail. When Sally wasn't relaying these to various departments, she was answering phone calls, fielding general enquiries and connecting callers to the correct extensions.

By the middle of her first week she'd made firm friends with Kim, a young Chinese-Australian girl who worked in the accounting department, and Maeve, a bubbly redheaded environmental field officer, who'd once worked out west and knew the country around Tarra-Binya.

There were moments when Sally missed home, when she felt nostalgic for the smell of gum trees…the chorus of early morning bird calls…the low throaty growl of her dad's tractor starting up…

But the homesickness didn't last long, especially as there was a park close to the office. She soon made a habit of walking through the park every morning and afternoon en route between the train station and the Blackcorp offices. In the middle of the park, the rumble of the traffic became muted and she could enjoy the gentle splashing of the fountain in the pond, the cooing of a hundred pigeons.

There were no *Keep off the grass* signs, thank heavens, and by the third afternoon she felt confident enough to take off her shoes so she could feel the soft, velvety lawn beneath her bare feet.

There were other people enjoying this green haven in the heart of the city too. Lovers, lost in each other's eyes. A hunched old man feeding crusts to the pigeons. Two fresh-faced schoolboys kicking a football.

The boys were playing with a man, their father perhaps, or an uncle. His clothes suggested that he worked in the city. He'd removed his jacket and tie, however, as well as his socks and shoes, and he'd rolled up the bottom of his trousers. Sally could see his discarded clothing, left rather nonchalantly on the ground beneath a shady tree, next to the boys' school bags.

The three males were having such fun, lunging spectacularly to take difficult catches, laughing and yelling instructions and showing off madly. They reminded Sally of her brothers playing in the garden with her dad, except…

Except…

Oh, good grief. The man was Logan Black.

She hadn't recognised him immediately because he looked so different without his jacket and tie and with that deliriously carefree grin on his face. He looked wonderful now, moving swiftly across the grass with the same spare, easy athleticism of an Outback horseman.

And then Logan Black saw Sally.

One of the boys had just sent him a high arching kick and he was running backwards, eyes up, on the ball, when his gaze flashed towards her. He seemed to freeze as his gaze met hers. His eyes widened as he recognised her. But then his attention quickly snapped back to the ball.

The small distraction, however, had cost him precious seconds and now he had to tear backwards, arms stretched back behind his head, to catch the football.

Reaching back…reaching…

Sally recognised the danger at the same moment as the boys cried, 'Uncle! Look out!'

'Watch the water!'

Their warnings were too late.

Just as Logan's fingers gripped the ball, he overbalanced, toppling backwards into the pond.

Sally didn't hesitate. She raced forward, her mind throwing up scary memories of her brothers' close calls in the creek at Tarra-Binya. Logan Black could hit his head on a submerged rock. He might become entangled in weed. Worst of all, he might not be able to swim.

By the time she reached the edge of the pond, however, Logan was already struggling to his feet. The water was only knee-deep and he hadn't dropped the football. Despite his dripping state, he held it triumphantly aloft, as if catching it were the most important thing in the world and ruining expensive Italian trousers counted for nothing.

Men!

Sally wanted to feel anger, was dismayed by the mad thumping of her heart, so different from the reaction of the boys, who rushed up beside her and immediately doubled over with helpless laughter. She had to admit it was an amazing sight—her *boss* standing knee-deep in water and drenched from head to toe.

But soon she was painfully aware of Logan's wet business shirt, rendered transparent by the water and now plastered against his skin. He might have been naked! She could see every detail of his tanned chest and the impressive bulk of his shoulders. She couldn't drag her eyes from the sight of his deeply sculpted muscles, the pleasing taper to his narrow hips.

Embarrassing heat flooded her.

'Hey, Uncle Logan, great save,' called one of the giggling boys.

Logan grinned back at them good-naturedly, threw the ball to the taller boy, then switched his gaze swiftly to Sally. He didn't speak as he stepped out of the pond, water streaming from his clothing.

Sally felt compelled to say something. 'I'm so glad you're all right, Mr Black. For a minute there, I thought I was going to have to dive in and rescue you.'

He grunted something incomprehensible and then his gaze travelled very deliberately downwards from Sally's hair to her shoes, which were dangling from her hand, and then to her bare feet. A corner of his mouth tilted, just a little, and his eyes seemed to blaze with black flames. Sally felt dizzy, as if she'd done too many cartwheels.

But then the unsettling light in his eyes suddenly died and his mouth flattened. Clearly he was extremely embarrassed to be caught dripping-wet and as good as naked in a public place. And in front of an employee.

Sally, equally embarrassed, dropped her gaze to her feet, which seemed to have become the focus of his attention. Thank heavens she'd given herself a pedicure at the weekend and painted her toenails a frosted berry colour.

He looked displeased, however, and she nervously fumbled with her shoes and struggled to slip them on. It was silly to be so self-conscious. Her bare feet weren't nearly as revealing as Logan's transparent shirt. Then again, she was still recovering from a nightmare incident, was still edgy with men.

To make matters worse, the schoolboys were watching her with marked curiosity.

'These are my nephews,' Logan explained, speaking with cold dignity befitting The Boss in An Awkward Situation. He didn't offer the boys' names.

Sally tried to sound cool. 'Hi guys.' To her dismay she sounded far too breathless.

'This is Miss…Miss…' Logan Black frowned and a muscle in his jaw twitched, but he covered his ignorance quickly. 'This young lady works at Blackcorp.'

Not for much longer, Sally thought miserably. She seemed to be doomed where this boss was concerned. First, her carelessness had pre-empted Rose's invasion of his office and now her appearance in the park had distracted him and caused this accident.

'Shall I pop back to the office and hunt down a towel, Mr Black?'

His frown deepened and he shook his head. 'No, no. That's kind of you, but there's no need.'

It was patently clear that he wanted her to disappear.

Sally took the cue. 'Well…I must get going or I'll miss my train.'

With a deliberately cheery wave for the boys, she hurried off, chin high and without a single glance back.

Logan watched her moving swiftly away from him, watched the bounce of her curls lit to a high sheen by the afternoon sun. Just as he'd anticipated, her hair was exceptionally pretty in the sunlight. Her feet were pretty too, so neatly shaped and smooth-skinned. As for the sway of her hips and the sexy curve of her—

'Do we have to go home already?'

His nephew's question pulled Logan back from the brink of an untimely fantasy. He glanced at his watch again, became acutely aware of his dripping clothes. A brisk breeze swept across the park and he felt suddenly cold. Time to snap to his senses.

He wondered suddenly what had come over him. How on earth had he allowed himself to be so distracted by his newest employee that he'd fallen in the pond? To make matters worse, he realised with some alarm that his decision to bring his sister's boys to the park had been inspired by the same girl.

When he'd seen her last week, on the day she'd applied for the front desk job, he'd sensed a special warmth and closeness between the young woman and the tiny girl and he'd been hit by a strangely inexplicable sense of loneliness—the loneliness of self-imposed isolation. Very soon after that he'd rung his sister, Carissa, knowing that it had been far too long since he'd seen her.

Now, as he drove the boys to their home, he tried to forget about the front desk girl. He suffered his sister's chuckling bewilderment when she saw his drenched clothes, but she was kind enough to offer him a hot shower and a pair of her husband Geoff's jeans and a T-shirt.

She offered him dinner too. Geoff had been delayed at work, so it was a noisy meal of chicken and pasta in Carissa's bright kitchen. Logan usually ate alone, defrosting his housekeeper's frozen meals in the microwave, and he couldn't remember the last time he'd enjoyed a relaxed, laughter-filled meal like this.

Several times, a picture of the girl in the park flashed into his thoughts. He wondered where she was dining tonight, then quickly scotched that thought. When Logan wanted a woman, he chose wisely from the ambitious and sophisticated businesswomen who were as keen to avoid emotional entanglements as he was.

He couldn't afford to be sidetracked. He had a five-year business plan which didn't allow for a dangerous flirtation with a girl fresh from the country with stars in her eyes.

Sally told herself that there was no sense in letting her mind go over and over this afternoon's encounter. But all evening her mind kept tossing up memories of her boss in the park. She kept seeing the look of unguarded happiness on Logan Black's face as he'd played with his nephews. She kept remembering the raw masculine appeal of his body beneath the wet shirt and the shocking heat of her response.

She shouldn't be feeling that way about her boss, didn't want to feel that way about any man. She was still getting over the painful lesson she'd learned on a summer's night at a ball in the Tarra-Binya Country Club's hall.

Her mistake, on that night, had been that she was too trusting, too friendly. Perhaps she'd also been a little too complacent.

She'd been to so many country dances that she'd felt completely at ease and in her element and, of course, she'd welcomed the added excitement of the newcomer, Kyle Francis.

Kyle was handsome, suntanned and tall, with a very trendy hairstyle that screamed *City Man*. He also had dreamy blue eyes, a very sexy smile and a glamorous movie star aura and he'd sent all the girls at the dance atwitter. But, almost as soon as he'd arrived, he'd made a beeline for Sally and she'd found it enormously flattering that he was only interested in her.

The dance music that evening had been fabulous—supplied by a band that had come all the way from Tamworth. Kyle had danced superbly and Sally had floated on happiness. She'd wondered later if his expensive aftershave had cast some kind of spell over her, because she'd been totally ensnared by his magnetic allure.

The evening had been so hot that all the doors and windows in the hall had been flung wide open to catch the slightest breeze, so it was incredibly easy to slip outside. Sally had been more than happy to let Kyle kiss her, and when he'd suggested that they take a stroll along the shadowy creek bank where she-oaks shielded them from view, she'd been too excited to pay attention to the niggling warnings of her common sense.

She'd never once encountered a problem with any of the local fellows. One or two had tried moves on her, of course, but things had never gone any further than she'd wanted them to. Besides, the local guys knew the Finch brothers would come down like a ton of bricks if anyone ever upset their baby sister.

Sally hadn't dreamed that Kyle planned to seduce her right then and there in the pine needle strewn earth of the river bank. She hadn't guessed that his charm would switch in a flash if he didn't get what he wanted.

But that had happened.

So quickly, the night had changed from a carefree evening of fun to one of stark terror and violence. Sally shuddered and cringed as the gruesome memories assaulted her now like physical blows.

She had to take deep steadying breaths as she pushed the nightmare images aside and told herself that all that was in the past. She was fine now. Steve had rescued her before any real harm was done and he'd sent Kyle Francis fleeing, never to return.

The family had closed ranks around Sally to protect her, of course, but finally she'd felt compelled to break free from her parents' and brothers' smothering concern. She'd come to Sydney to claim her independence, but she would achieve this much more readily if she remembered that Logan Black was her boss. No more, no less.

At work the next morning, one of the special couriers was leaning casually against Sally's desk, one elbow on the counter top while he quizzed her about her plans for the coming weekend, when clipped footsteps marched across the marble foyer, then stopped.

She looked up to find Logan Black standing stock still. To her dismay, she felt her cheeks grow hot.

'M-Mr Black.' She managed to smile. 'Good morning.'

He didn't respond, just stood there, looking grim.

'Was there something you wanted?' she asked. 'Can I help?'

Again, he didn't answer, simply let his relentless gaze sweep over Brett, the courier, before shooting a pointed glance at the clock on the wall.

Brett got the message and beat a hasty retreat. Finally, the boss spoke. 'I have an important visitor arriving at ten o'clock. Charles Holmes, the CEO of Minmount Mining.'

Everything about his manner was aloof and businesslike as if the football game and the tumble into the pond had never happened.

Sally lifted her chin. This was good. Much better to have a proud and distant boss than one who flirted. 'I'll look out for Mr Holmes,' she assured him.

Logan nodded. 'Charles knows his way about this place and he certainly doesn't need an identity tag but, as a courtesy, I'd like you to escort him to my office. Maria Paige, my PA, will take over from there.'

'Of course, Mr Black. I'll see to that. No problem.'

He nodded coolly, then turned to swipe his electronic card before proceeding through the security doors.

Shortly before ten o'clock, an absolutely gorgeous bouquet of snowy-white roses arrived and Sally's imagination kicked in straight away. It was someone's birthday. The flowers were for one of the female employees from an admirer. Already, she was anticipating the enjoyment of taking the flowers through to the person's office, watching the surprised pleasure on her face.

Oh, she loved this job.

But when she looked for the usual small white envelope, she couldn't find one. She frowned at the delivery boy. 'There's no card here. Nothing to say who the flowers are for.'

He shrugged. 'No need. They're for Mr Black.'

'*Mr* Black?'

The delivery boy nodded, his expression blank, as if there was nothing unusual about a man receiving flowers.

'Oh. I—I see.' Straightening her shoulders, Sally secured a pleasant smile. 'Lovely. I'll take them up to him.'

The lift was filled with the delicate scent of roses as she ascended to the next floor. She closed her eyes, drew a deep breath of sweetly perfumed air and gave herself yet another stern lecture. Here, in her arms, was the indisputable evidence that her boss had a private life that included a woman. At last, she had a very, *very* good reason to put him right out of her head.

Maria Paige, the boss's PA, looked up without smiling as Sally approached her desk just outside Logan's office. She was one of the few employees at Blackcorp who'd hadn't bothered to be friendly.

'Oh, the roses,' she said. 'Good. Pop them in the vase there.'

A large vase already filled with water was ready and waiting at one end of Maria's desk.

'You must have been expecting these,' Sally said as she lowered the roses carefully into the vase.

Maria shot a sharp glance over the top of her glasses. 'Yes, of course. They come every Friday.'

'Really? Someone sends the boss flowers every week?' Sally, super-aware of the open doorway to Logan's office, spoke in a stage whisper.

'Mr Black has a standing order with the florist,' Maria said impatiently. 'He takes them with him every Friday evening.'

So the *boss* was the admirer, not the admiree.

Sally knew this was none of her business. Logan Black had every right to buy flowers each week for the woman he loved. In actual fact, she was very pleased by the news that he was 'taken' because it meant she had absolutely nothing to fear from him.

She might have asked the reluctant Maria more questions,

but the PA's attention was distracted by the arrival of a tall, imposing, silver-haired man in a dark business suit.

'Mr Holmes,' Maria said with a suddenly animated smile, 'I'll tell Mr Black that you're here.'

As Maria lifted a phone and murmured into it, Sally's stomach became a lead weight crashing to the floor. This was Charles Holmes, the important businessman she was supposed to escort up here. Someone else must have let him in and he'd found his own way.

She thought about trying to escape before her slackness was discovered but, from behind her, she heard the boss's voice.

'Charles, good to see you.' Logan Black came out of his office, his hand extended to welcome his guest. Sally was riveted to the spot.

As soon as the two men had greeted each other, the boss half-turned and gave her a brief nod.

'Thanks, Miss Sparrow.'

The fact that he'd got her name wrong, yet again, didn't bother her nearly so much as the knowledge that she hadn't carried out his request.

This was the first tiny task Logan had assigned her and she'd failed. If she hadn't been so distracted by the arrival of his roses, she would have remembered that Charles Holmes was coming at ten. If she hadn't been so busy quizzing Maria about the bouquet, she might have been back at her desk when Mr Holmes had arrived.

'You got away with that,' Maria said snakily as the men disappeared into Logan's office. 'But you'd better make sure it never happens again.'

Grateful that Maria hadn't revealed her failure and feeling several versions of guilty, Sally hurried away. This mistake was yet another very clear sign that she had to focus one hundred per cent on her job. Not her boss.

Midafternoon Janet Keaton provided a welcome distraction when she called at Sally's desk with the personality questionnaire.

'Drop it back on my desk when you're done,' she told Sally. 'It will be helpful for next week's team-building workshop.'

'Will I be involved?'

'Yes.' Janet smiled at her. 'New employees can be very helpful in these situations. You haven't been indoctrinated yet by the office culture. Lucy from my office will look after your desk for the day. Everyone is to meet in the conference room at nine o'clock on Tuesday morning.'

CHAPTER FOUR

SALLY was relieved to see Maeve's friendly face as soon as she walked into the conference room on Tuesday morning. Her new friend waved to catch her attention and patted a spare chair beside her.

A cross section of employees was there—everyone from department heads to Sally, the lowly newcomer—and, to her pleased surprise, she was able to recognise nearly everybody by sight, if not by name. More than one person sent her a friendly smile or wave.

Janet Keaton called them to order. 'I'd like to break the ice by giving you a chance to get to know each other better. You'll find marker pens and a blank name-plate in front of you and I want you to fill in your names.'

A small babble of good-natured chatter rippled around the room as people picked up pens, but the noise died and heads turned as a tall, commanding figure strode into the room.

'Ah, Mr Black.' Janet met her boss's stern frown with a warm smile. 'I'm so glad you could join us.'

Join us? Sally's jaw fell so hard she was surprised it didn't hit the desk.

'There's a spare seat here, Logan,' Janet said. 'I saved it especially for you.'

The boss took the seat Janet indicated next to Hank James, the company's Information Technology guru. He thumbed a button to open his jacket, crossed one long black-trousered leg over the other and scanned the room with a haughty, narrow-eyed gaze.

Annoying lightning flashes strafed through Sally and she wondered miserably how she was going to throw off these ridiculous reactions to her employer.

'What a pity,' Maeve muttered out of the side of her mouth. 'Just when we were ready to have fun.'

'The boss won't spoil the fun, will he?' Sally hissed back.

'He's pretty cool, actually,' Maeve admitted. 'In a remote and godlike kind of way. A bit out of our league.'

'Fill in your name-plate, please,' Janet told Logan. 'In case anyone here doesn't know you.' She chuckled as she made this small joke, and there was a smattering of polite laughter.

Janet beamed at everyone. 'Now, if you turn the name-plates over, you'll find a word written under it.'

'Here we go,' muttered Maeve. 'Party time.' She grinned as she turned over her name-plate. 'Oh, sweet. I'm Cinderella.'

Sally laughed. 'I'm Butter.'

'OK,' said Janet. 'I want you to mingle and chat until you find a partner whose name links with yours. For example, if you were given the name Salt, you'll need to find Pepper.'

Maeve chuckled. 'Ripper. I'm off to find Prince Charming.'

Laughter and chatter filled the room as everyone wandered about, greeting people and trying to find their match.

'I suppose I'm looking for Butterfly,' Josie, the company's solicitor, told Sally. 'I'm Caterpillar.'

'Maybe you should be looking for Leaf?' Sally suggested.

Hank, the gentle, bespectacled IT guy, was Wolf. 'You wouldn't be Red Riding Hood, would you, Sally?'

'Sorry.'

She studiously avoided Logan Black, but she was constantly aware of his tall, dark-suited presence in her peripheral vision. He seemed to mix quite easily with his staff, which made her wonder about his customary indifference to her.

Before very long, couples found each other—Apple and Orange, Merry and Christmas, Romeo and Juliet. There was no obvious pairing of males with females, but Prince Charming turned out to be a rather hunky suntanned young geologist. Maeve sent Sally a wink and looked as pleased as a cat with more than her share of the cream.

Eventually everyone had paired up except Sally, and she found herself left in the middle of the room, feeling just a little foolish and self-conscious.

'Haven't you found a partner?' Janet asked her.

She shrugged and shook her head. 'There doesn't seem to be anyone here who matches with Butter.'

A strangely tense silence fell over the group and Sally wondered if everyone else in the room knew something she didn't.

'That would be me,' said a deep male voice from behind her.

She spun around and pins and needles danced over her skin as she met the cool, dark eyes of Logan Black. He smiled ever so faintly as he held up his name-plate and revealed one word: *Bread*.

'Well, there you go!' Janet looked delighted and actually clapped her hands.

Sally forced her face muscles to form a smile.

'I want you to go off in your pairs. Move the chairs if you like. Or go next door to the canteen. Find somewhere private to sit where you can talk. In HR circles, we call this activity *Blind Date*. You have twenty minutes to get to know as much as you can about each other.'

It was a simple request and everyone else looked happy to

pair up and find a place to sit. Maeve and her young geologist were already in a far corner, grinning stupidly at each other and clearly getting on like a bushfire.

Logan Black, however, made no attempt to approach Sally and she remained marooned in the middle of the room.

She'd never been a wallflower at a dance, but now she knew exactly how those poor girls had felt. If the boss was going to be stuffy about this, she might hold her head high and sweep out of the room.

'Come on, you two.' Janet was like a mother hen shooing her chicks. 'Off you go. Get cracking with the questions.'

To Sally's dismay, Logan Black stuck his jaw at a belligerent angle and approached Janet, dipped his head and muttered something in her ear.

Sally could guess what the boss was saying: he didn't want to be teamed with the newest, lowliest employee.

But Janet dismissed him with a wave of her hand. 'These sorts of exercises are never a waste of time. This will be good for you, Logan. You're an introverted thinking type and Sally's an extroverted feeling type. It's a perfect match. Now off you go. Think of it as a blind date and be a good sport.'

Sally knew her cheeks were bright pink, but she was not going to let the boss upset her. Lifting her chin, she smiled at him bravely. 'I'm ready when you are, Mr Black.'

'Very well,' he said grimly and his frown deepened as he nodded to a vacant table with two chairs. 'Over here will do, Miss—'

With a shrewd smile, Sally turned her name-plate over.

'Ah, yes. Miss Finch. Not Sparrow.'

It was a small victory and she wished she felt more relaxed as she sat, hoping her heart and lungs would behave normally as Logan Black lowered his long frame into a chair on the other side of the small desk that separated them.

She drew some comfort from Janet's suggestion that the boss was an introverted thinking type. It made sense. She'd met men like him before, in the Outback. Quiet, almost reclusive men, driven by inner goals.

Now he said, with an affectation of boredom, 'Ladies first. Apparently, you have to tell me all about yourself.'

'What would you like to know?'

His eyebrows were black and perfectly arched and, in response to her question, the right one lifted. 'How are you settling in to your work here?'

'I think I've settled in rather quickly. I love working here.'

'That's good to hear.'

To cover the awkward silence that followed, Sally said, 'I guess it's my turn to ask you a question.'

'Fire away.'

'What did you have for breakfast?'

'I beg your pardon?'

Logan couldn't have looked more stunned if Sally had asked for his home telephone number.

'I—I asked what you had for breakfast.'

'What kind of a question is that?'

'A safe one, I hope.'

He smiled.

Oh, my gosh. When he smiled the skin around his eyes crinkled and his face was transformed. He looked just as he had playing football with his nephews—delightfully carefree and young.

'I had a cup of coffee for breakfast,' he said.

'Is that all?'

'Yes. It's all I ever have.'

Sally was sure she shouldn't correct her boss, but she couldn't help herself. 'But breakfast is terribly important. My father and brothers couldn't face a day's work without a mountain of toast and a full cooked breakfast.'

'What kinds of work do your father and brothers do?'

'Is that your next question?'

Another gorgeous smile. 'I guess it is.'

Emboldened by this warmth, Sally told him, 'My father and my eldest brother, Matt, run our family's sheep and wheat property at Tarra-Binya. Steve's on an oil rig off Western Australia. Josh operates a big drag line in the Central Queensland coalfields and Damon's a mustering contractor, when he's not on the rodeo circuit.'

The dark eyebrows rose higher while she told him this. 'That's quite a family. I can see why they need their big breakfasts.'

Sally smiled. 'And now it's my turn to ask another question.'

Logan Black actually chuckled. 'I'm nervous.'

'Don't be.' She stifled a terrible urge to ask him about the white roses. *I can't ask that. I mustn't.* Instead, she blurted, 'What's the most important thing I should know about you?'

'I'm your boss.'

'Come on, that's cheating. It has to be something I don't already know.'

'Who said there were rules?'

'We're supposed to be getting to know each other.' The sudden tightness in Logan's face warned Sally that she might be overstepping the mark. 'Of course, you're right. You're the boss and you should set the rules.'

He accepted this as his due. 'I'm sure we're not supposed to get deep and meaningful. Stick to everyday, non-invasive questions. Ask me whether I've lived in Sydney all my life, or where I went to school. Favourite subjects at school. That sort of thing.'

'Let me guess. Your favourite subject at school was mathematics.'

A surprised little laugh escaped him. 'Absolutely.'

'And you went to a private boys' school like Sydney Grammar or King's.'

Again, he looked amused. 'Almost right. I started at Sydney Grammar, but—' he dropped his gaze and released a rough sigh 'my family fell on hard times and I couldn't stay there.'

'That's rotten luck.' The grim set of his mouth told Sally that this had been a huge disappointment. 'You've obviously done very well in spite of the setback,' she suggested gently.

Shrugging her sympathy aside, as if he wanted to get away from the subject of his family's misfortune, he said, 'But I *have* lived in Sydney all my life.' He looked up again. 'I guess you must have spent most of your life out west.'

She told him briefly about Tarra-Binya and even more briefly about Chloe. She said, 'I know you like football. What's your favourite?'

At first he looked upset and Sally wondered if she'd broken an unspoken rule. Were they really supposed to pretend that the interlude in the park had never happened?

After a bit, he said simply, 'I really like Rugby League.' And then, 'What about you? What sports do you play?'

'I've given most of them a go,' she told him. 'But I guess I was best at tennis and horse riding.' She watched him thoughtfully. 'So you were good at school, good at sport and you're successful in your career. Is there anything you're not good at?'

He laughed and had the grace to look embarrassed. 'Oh, yes. I'm absolutely hopeless at dancing.'

'Really?' Sally gasped—not because Logan's answer was so surprising, but because her heart began to race and a wave of fear rose through her as she remembered that horrifying night at the country dance. She saw again Kyle Francis's handsome face, his beguiling smile as he'd coaxed her outside.

It's OK. I can do this. She was not going to panic simply because a man mentioned the word *dancing*.

Logan was looking puzzled and he sounded defensive. 'Most guys are hopeless at dancing, aren't they?'

OK…she could either dissolve into a nervous heap or she could rise above this moment. Knowing she'd rather not dissolve, Sally held her head high. 'Where I come from, everyone goes to bush dances and Outback balls. My big brothers taught me how to dance. The waltz, the samba, the foxtrot. I love to dance!'

Wow, she'd said it. On a wave of euphoria, she added gleefully, 'Dancing's not that hard.'

'I don't believe you.'

'Even I could teach someone like you.'

Oh, cringe. Now she was getting carried away. In the awkward pause that followed, she half-expected the boss to retaliate by asking her what she was bad at, but he was obviously too polite.

'Here's an everyday, non-invasive question,' she said, hurrying, before the silence became too much. 'What kind of music do you like?'

She was surprised by the evident pleasure in his face. 'That's easy. I like all sorts of music. My grandmother was a classical pianist and I guess I've inherited her love of music but, unfortunately, none of her talent.'

This was a layer to the boss Sally hadn't anticipated, but at least they'd stopped talking about dancing.

'I don't know much at all about classical music,' she admitted. 'Chloe used to take me to concerts though, and since I've been living in her house I've been listening to her CDs. They're mostly classical or jazz and some of them are just gorgeous.'

'Is there any one piece you particularly like?'

'Well…' She paused. She'd never had a serious discussion about music and she felt a tad pretentious. 'I've discovered an amazing violin concerto. It's kind of uplifting and sad and joyful all at once.'

'Which composer?' Logan was suddenly alert, leaning forward, his dark eyes keenly focused on her.

'Brahms.'

'Ah, yes,' he said softly, almost reverently, and, for no reason that she could explain, fine hairs lifted on Sally's arms. 'The Brahms violin concerto is one of my favourites too.'

'The music's so powerful,' she said. 'And there's a passage towards the end of the first movement.'

'Where the music suddenly slows down?'

'Yes, it's so beautiful. There's such a depth of feeling.'

Logan nodded. 'You have to stop everything and just listen.'

'And it touches you deep inside in a way that's impossible to put into words.'

Her boss was looking at her now with an expression of such intense fascination that Sally, without warning, felt as if she wanted to cry.

'Goodness,' she said, blinking quickly and trying to make light of the moment. 'We almost got deep and meaningful there. And you said that's against the rules.'

He smiled slowly, almost sadly.

'We'd better think of another question,' she said. 'What about travel?'

For a moment, Sally had the distinct impression that he would have preferred to continue talking about music, but then, with a little shrug, he asked, 'Have you travelled?'

'Not outside Australia. But I'm very keen to go overseas.'

Logan had relaxed again, sitting with an elbow hooked over the back of his chair. 'If you only had the opportunity to travel to one place overseas, where would it be?'

She grinned at him. 'You're really getting into the swing of this.'

'Answer the question, Miss Finch.'

'*And* you remembered my surname.' She looked down and saw that he'd read her name-plate. With a cunning smile, she said, 'One place overseas? Let me see. I think that would have to be Paris. I'd love to see the Seine and the Champs-Elysées.'

She hesitated, frowning. 'No, wait a minute. I think, if I can only have one place, it would have to be in Italy. Florence or Venice. Yes, I think I'd definitely choose Venice.' Chloe had so many beautiful photographs of the canals. All those gorgeous arched bridges and the gondolas and the old crumbling buildings. 'Everything there is so full of history.'

'Brahms loved Vienna.'

'Well, Vienna would be good too. Oh, hang, I don't think I could ever settle for just one place.'

Sally grinned and Logan grinned back at her and the world seemed, suddenly, to be a brighter and more beautiful place.

'Are you two still chatting?'

They turned to find Janet Keaton bearing down on them.

'Didn't you hear me? Time's well and truly up.'

Sally looked about her and realised that all the others were back in their places and were watching the two of them with wry amusement.

'We were late starting,' Logan muttered smoothly and then he stood and was very dignified as he returned to his seat next to Hank without a backward glance at Sally.

Not surprisingly, Janet now wanted everyone to introduce the person they'd interviewed to the whole group, sharing what they'd discovered about that person.

Logan hardly heard what they others said. He was too busy trying to work out why his newest employee had such a disturbing effect on him. She was pretty, certainly, but not as beautiful as many of the women he'd dated.

Those golden curls continued to intrigue him, but it was

more than that. Sally Finch radiated warmth and vitality and there was something very wide-eyed and fresh about her that stirred memories of the strangest things—the first exciting day of the long summer holidays, waking as a child on Christmas morning.

He'd never met a woman quite like her. But he wasn't going to admit that here. In the end, when it was his turn to introduce Sally, he spoke simply about her family, about her country girlhood and her desire to travel. He certainly didn't mention the moment of spine-tingling connection while they'd been talking about the Brahms. For him, it was one of those rare experiences, like the music, that remained beyond the reach of mere words.

He wondered if Sally would mention it when she introduced him. As she got to her feet, he was on tenterhooks, fearful that this outspoken young woman might reveal too much about their conversation. But, to his surprise, Sally was extremely circumspect. His business CV was more personally revealing than her careful introduction.

Janet Keaton caught his eye, her expression faintly bewildered. What had she expected? That Sally would spill one of his deep, dark secrets?

Perhaps they'd both underestimated the newest employee.

For Sally, the rest of the workshop was every bit as much fun as she'd anticipated. There were all sorts of problem-solving exercises which brought out different people's strengths and weaknesses and showed the benefits of working in a team. She found that she was a lateral thinker, good at listening and at being empathetic, but she wasn't so hot when it came to logic and spatial skills.

In groups, they hunted for errors in messages, tried to find triangles inside pentagons and to draw circle-and-dot diagrams without taking their pens off the paper. There were even moments of self-disclosure where they shared fantasies.

Sally's fantasy was to have long, straight, dark hair. The boss surprised everyone, except Sally, by claiming that he would love to have played Rugby League for Australia.

Logan disappeared at lunch time and missed the rather delicious smorgasbord served in the dining room.

Maeve pounced on Sally. 'Poor you. What was it like being grilled by the boss?'

'Nerve-racking until he thawed out. Then he was close to normal.'

'I must say you looked pretty into each other by the end.'

Sally tried to make light of it. 'We were just talking about travel. How was Prince Charming?'

'Fabulous.' Maeve's eyes danced with excitement. 'I'm going out with him tonight.'

'Tonight?' Sally gaped at her friend. 'Wow! That was quick work.'

Maeve grinned happily. 'Our chat session was as good as a date. A kind of blind date in the workplace.'

In a strange way, so was mine, Sally thought. *Good grief.* What would Logan say if he could read her thoughts?

Now she really was getting carried away.

The boss returned in time for the afternoon session. They were broken into competitive teams and given a kit of materials and instructed to build an 'anti-grenade' that would protect the shell of an egg. The time limit was thirty minutes.

Sally was hopeless at this and happy to cheer on her team mates. After they'd built their device from reinforced cardboard and crumpled paper, they went to a 'test site' in the park, where they had to throw their constructions.

Sally's team broke their egg.

The boss's team won, launching their device the furthest distance and keeping the egg intact.

He hadn't been in Sally's team for any of the day's team activities, and he'd paid her no attention, but during the entire time she was ridiculously super-aware of him. It was awful, like having a high school crush on a senior boy, but so much more painful because it was so pointless.

Because it wasn't supposed to happen.

After a scrumptious afternoon tea of scones with strawberry jam and cream, along with piping-hot tea, Janet announced that it was time to draw some conclusions from the day's activities.

'But, before that,' she said, 'I'd like you to return to the pairs you were in this morning, when we had that first ice-breaker session.'

Sally's stomach tightened. From across the room, she saw Logan stiffen and glance her way. But his expression remained deadpan as he beckoned to her to come and join him.

Flashing hot and cold, she crossed the room.

'This time, I'm going to give you a list of questions,' Janet said as she moved between their tables, distributing sheets of paper. 'Feedback from others is the most important form of reality check we can have. It's a matter of lowering your façades and seeing yourselves as others see you and it's very illuminating self-knowledge.'

Sally cringed. Receiving feedback from her boss would be bad enough, but giving it would be incredibly risky!

With trepidation, she read the questions on the sheet.

What was your first impression of me?
Why did you have that impression?
Who did I remind you of? Why?
How accurate do you now think that impression was?

Ouch! How could she be honest about her first impression? She'd met Logan Black on the day of the interview when he'd found Rose under his desk and she'd thought he was an arrogant prig.

Looking up at him now, she saw a dark red stain creep up his neck. *He's as uncomfortable with this as I am.* She dropped her gaze to her hands and twisted them nervously.

Logan made a small throat-clearing sound. 'Trust Janet to save the punchline for last.' He shot Sally a piercing look from beneath half-lowered lids. 'Would you like to start?'

She tried to smile and failed. 'I'd rather not.'

Drawing back an immaculate white cuff, he looked at his watch, which was, of course, beautiful and gold and very expensive-looking. 'Actually, I'm not sure we can do this. I have a meeting at four.

'Yes, you mustn't miss your meeting.' Sally was as glad to escape as he was.

Logan stood, but Janet Keaton was too quick for them.

'I hope you're not planning to wriggle out of this, Logan,' she said, loudly enough for several others to hear.

'I have an important meeting at four,' he said, jaw jutting at a distinctly antagonistic angle.

'That's fine. You still have plenty of time for a quick recap.'

Sally waited for Logan to pull rank and to insist that he couldn't possibly stay. It would be dead easy for him to leave now. But, to her surprise, he caught her eye and smiled conspiratorially. 'I guess we'd better do as we're told.'

As Janet moved away, he sat down again, rested his elbows on the desk and leaned closer to Sally. 'Don't look so worried, Sally. I'm not going to eat you. As a matter of fact, I'm prepared to admit straight out that my first impression of you was completely off track.'

Sally gulped. 'Really?'

'I assumed you were a single mother,' he said. 'And a rather careless one at that.'

'When I was actually a careless aunt,' she suggested with a small smile.

The responding warmth in his eyes sent a sweet shiver over her arms. She was about to comment that Logan seemed to enjoy his role as an uncle when he asked, 'How is the little boy who had the asthma attack?'

Sally swallowed her surprise. She had no idea her boss knew about Oliver. 'He's much better, thank you. They've put him on some kind of preventative medicine that seems to be doing the trick.'

Logan nodded, then looked down at the sheet of questions. 'I'm expected to say who you remind me of.'

'Please don't say a corn cob.'

'Why on earth would I say that?'

'It's what my brothers called me. And then everyone at school.'

'Because of your hair?'

Sally sighed. 'You guessed it.'

His gaze rested on her hair for longer than was necessary, but he made no comment. 'Actually, you're rather like my sister, Carissa,' he said. 'You're totally different physically, but she has the same kind of vibrancy as you.'

Vibrancy? The boss thought she was vibrant?

'And you like to talk. You and Carissa both *really* like to talk.'

He glanced again at the question sheet. Without looking at Sally, he said, 'But I must admit that my recent impressions have been more favourable than my first one.'

Sally was rather pleased that he didn't look up to see her blush.

'And now it's your turn.' He smiled at her gently. 'Don't be too brutal.'

'And risk getting sacked?' She gave a shaky laugh. 'I wouldn't dare.'

'But there's no point in being dishonest.'

Sally swallowed, took a deep breath. 'OK. My first impression was that you were—er—very big and dark.' When his expression remained blank she quickly added, 'And I also got the strong impression that you didn't like children.'

'Good heavens.' He looked genuinely shocked.

'You were holding poor little Rose away from you as if she might be infectious.'

He dismissed this with a shrug. 'I'm not used to babies.'

'Since then, of course, I've realised that was wrong. You're wonderful with your nephews.' She waited for him to frown or show displeasure that she'd mentioned this. When he did neither, she said bravely, 'I've noticed that you're always super-busy and nearly always very serious.'

'That's true.'

'I thought you might not be very happy. Perhaps a bit lonely.'

He frowned at her.

'But then the roses arrived,' she said carefully.

'Roses?'

'The white roses that come every Friday.'

'Oh, yes, of course.'

'And I realised there must be someone very special in your life.'

A faint smile tilted the corners of his mouth.

'And, if that's the case—' She paused and swallowed. 'If there is someone special, then I'm sure you *must* be happy.'

His eyes, as he regarded her, were so thoughtful that Sally wondered what she'd said wrong. She glanced down quickly. 'What's the next question?'

'Who do I remind you of? And why?'

'Oh, yes.' She'd never really known many men from the

city. There'd been that one, of course, who'd caused her so much grief. But he'd been oozing smiles and pseudo-charm and Logan, thank heavens, was absolutely nothing like him.

'Actually, you remind me of quite a lot of people,' she said eventually. 'Men I've grown up with. Graziers, head stock-men, gun shearers. You have the same kind of confidence and inner drive. I'm guessing that you're very goal oriented.'

'And I'd say you're right.'

'My first impression wasn't accurate at all,' she admitted. 'You were very different—' She paused and took a deep breath. Perhaps she shouldn't mention how he'd looked during that memorable moment just before he'd fallen in the pond. Or this morning when he'd been talking about music. Instead, she said, 'I think you have a softer side that you try to hide.'

Predictably, Logan frowned again.

'But that's OK.' Sally knew she was skating on very thin ice, but the workshop was nearly over and she was feeling rather reckless. 'I guess a boss has to pretend to be tough.'

'It's not a matter of pretence. A boss *has* to be tough. It goes with the territory.' Logan glanced again at his watch and stood quickly. His eyes took on a kind of hooded hardness. 'Now, if you'll kindly excuse me, I really must go to this meeting.'

CHAPTER FIVE

IT HAD been the weirdest day.

Logan drove rather recklessly to his meeting, jumping lanes and taking corners too fast as his head reeled from the conversation he'd just had with his newest employee. Team-building was all very well—he had to admit he'd gained a new respect for many employees today—but he couldn't believe he'd revealed so much of his inner self to Sally Finch.

Allowing a glimpse beneath his careful façade was completely out of character. And to the front desk girl of all people!

And then, what cheek on Sally's part to suggest that he was not as tough as he made out. It was utter rubbish!

At the age of fifteen, when his father had gone bankrupt, he'd developed a super-tough outer shell. Since then, he'd hardened even more, had done everything in his power to make sure he never repeated his father's mistakes.

The traffic lights changed to red just in front of Logan, forcing him to brake sharply. Fingers tapping impatiently on the steering wheel, he watched pedestrians swarm across the crossing—men in business suits, schoolgirls in straw hats and navy-blue uniforms and a family of tourists in jeans and T-shirts.

Through narrowed eyes, Logan watched the tourists—

parents with two kids, a boy and a girl. The father's arm was draped loosely around his son's shoulders and, as they reached the safety of the opposite footpath, they seemed to share a joke.

Logan and his dad had been close like that.

The traffic lights changed again and Logan accelerated. He drove to the meeting on autopilot, his mind lodged in the past, on the lessons he'd learned from his father.

Dan Black had been loved by everyone for his hail-fellow-well-met bonhomie and it went without saying that Logan had also adored him and looked up to him as his hero. During the football season, they'd gone to every home game, the two of them dressed in the red and green colours of their adored team, the South Sydney Rabbitohs.

Back then, Logan had been blissfully unaware of the dangers of his father's impulsive, happy-go-lucky nature. It was only later that he'd understood the perils that came when a man's heart ruled his head.

Dan Black used to joke that he was the most successful businessman he knew who didn't work to a business plan.

Who needs strategies, son? Follow your heart and you'll always be right.

Sure, Dad.

For a while Dan Black had done well in real estate. Until there'd been a downturn. He'd come up with a grand scheme for aquaculture and set up a fish farm on the north coast. Six months later it had been wiped out by disease. Another dream, growing hydrangeas for the cut flower market, had been shattered by a hailstorm. Dan hadn't been insured.

The problem was clear to Logan now. His father had never focused on the main game. He'd never been prepared for potential problems, hadn't researched projects carefully, and his cash reserves had always been too low, so he hadn't been able to afford insurance, or to hedge against downturns.

After the final disaster, when Dan had been declared bankrupt, he'd collapsed with a complete nervous breakdown. He'd let his family and his investors down. Friendships had collapsed because Dan had eloquently persuaded pals to invest. Some had actually borrowed money to help him with his disastrous projects.

Logan and his sister had been forced to leave their private schools in the middle of term. Their teachers had been terribly upset, which had only added to their mortification.

Only their mother had adapted quickly to the changes the family had faced. Happily giving up her social life of tennis and bridge parties, she had taken lowly office jobs, intensifying Dan's humiliation by working for their friends.

The lesson for Logan had been crystal clear and painfully personal. Men who led with their hearts rather than their heads brought humiliation and hardship on the people they loved. It was absolutely vital to be disciplined, to put one hundred and ten per cent into studies and planning and business.

To make this happen, Logan had devised his five-year plan. Only when his finances were secure and he'd reached the very top of his game would he relax and allow himself to think about starting a family of his own.

He wondered now, as he drove into an underground car park, if he should have told Sally Finch about his plan. She'd given him the perfect opening when she'd suggested he was goal oriented. Perhaps he should have told her then exactly what his goals were and what he was prepared to give up while achieving them.

That would have stilled her tongue. He doubted she would have continued then about his hidden softness.

In retrospect, he wished he'd been honest, was surprised that he hadn't been.

Then again, he thought with a wry smile, revealing exactly

how tough he was might have snuffed out the dancing lights in Sally's eyes.

A man would have to be criminally insane to do that.

That evening, for the first time since she'd come to Sydney, Sally felt strangely unhappy and restless. Lonely too and just a little homesick.

How annoying.

She had been dead set on proving to herself and to her family that she was 'cured'. And today she'd taken an important step—she hadn't shied away from the conversation about dancing. She should be celebrating. She'd won a major battle with that particular demon.

Actually, she'd achieved many of her goals already. She had an interesting job, money coming in, new friends. Everything would be perfect if her boss were old and grey and happily married with a family.

OK...face the truth, Sally. Logan Black is your problem.

How silly. It was bad enough that she'd been smitten by the boss's good looks ever since that first sight of him on the day she'd applied for the job. But now, after their long and intimate conversations, she couldn't stop thinking about him. Not for a second. He was a man of such intriguing contradictions.

Today she'd caught glimpses into all sorts of interesting facets of his personality.

Stop it, Sally. Stop it now! He's out of bounds.

Promising herself for the hundred and fiftieth time that she would put the boss right out of her mind, she cooked up a big bowl of comforting pasta and poured a glass of white wine. Rather than eating alone at the kitchen table, she took her meal through to the lounge room, where she drew the pretty floral curtains and turned on the pink lampshades.

Usually, this room with its thick cream carpet, its lovely paintings and welcoming cushiony sofas lifted her spirits as soon as she entered it, but tonight the lovely house wouldn't—or couldn't—work its magic.

Sally knew it would be foolish to listen to the Brahms concerto tonight when she was trying, desperately, to forget about Logan Black, but in the end she was too weak to resist the temptation.

Curled in one of Chloe's squishy armchairs, she ate the pasta and drank her wine while the lush sounds of the gorgeous music swelled to fill the room.

I'm an idiot.

She longed for Chloe to be alive and here with her. She could picture her godmother sitting on the sofa in one of her bright kaftans with her silver hair piled gloriously on top of her head, a warm smile at the ready, as she offered sage advice.

But Chloe was gone and Sally was alone and she didn't want to ring her mother. Her mother was too attuned to her every mood and she would know immediately that something was wrong, and Sally was supposed to be proving that she was fine on her own.

With a heavy sigh, she turned her thoughts to Maeve, who was out tonight on a date with her young geologist.

How sensible of Maeve to be going out with one of the many friendly and unattached young fellows at Blackcorp. Sally knew that was exactly what she should be doing. Already, several friendly young men had stopped by her desk.

Why couldn't she have been smitten by one of them instead of dreaming about their aloof and unattainable boss, who hurried past her desk with more important things on his mind and bought white roses for another woman?

To make Sally's downbeat mood worse, the music

reached the especially beautiful passage she'd tried, so inadequately, to describe to Logan today. She remembered the tender expression in his eyes and tears rolled helplessly down her cheeks.

When the phone rang she almost left it, believing herself too maudlin for any kind of conversation. But, at the last gasp, she dived out of her chair, swiped at her damp cheeks and lifted the receiver.

'Oh, Sally,' cried Anna's voice, 'I'm so glad you're home. You see, Steve got back today and we were hoping to have a night out while he's on leave. Is there any chance you could mind Oliver and Rose on Friday evening?'

Sally assured her sister-in-law that she'd love to mind the children. And then, wanting to throw off any Cinderella-like sensibilities, she climbed the stairs and filled the bath with hot water and a quarter of a bottle of Chloe's expensive and utterly self-indulgent bath oil.

It was a night for pampering.

Logan sat in darkness in his penthouse apartment overlooking Sydney Harbour, watching the spectacle of lights reflected on the silky black water below while he listened to Brahms.

He tried to listen without thinking about Sally Finch. It was crazy that he was still thinking about her. But he kept picturing her here in his apartment, curled comfortably beside him on the sofa, her head resting on his shoulder as they listened to this music together. He imagined running his fingers through her dazzling curls.

Fool.

With an angry cry, he lurched to his feet and stood at the big picture window with his hands plunged deep in his pockets, staring hard at the inky water and the reflections of city lights while he willed his thoughts away from X-rated possibilities.

Sally Finch was an employee and he was a boss who never mixed business with his private life. He'd seen other men follow that course, only to run their businesses off track, or to crash on the sharp and treacherous rocks of office politics.

But, all that aside, Sally wasn't his type. With no professional qualifications, no burning ambition, no long-term plans, she'd drifted into an inheritance and found herself an easy job where she could chat all day.

In fact, she had too much to say. *I thought you might not be very happy.*

Her comments still nagged at him.

How could he *not* be happy? His life was at the exact place he wanted it to be. His business plan was on target, he had an enviable apartment with position, position, position. Women—beautiful, intelligent women—found him attractive. He was perfectly happy.

Today he'd told Sally that she reminded him of his sister and he had been dead right. Carissa had said something equally annoying last week when he'd dropped off the boys. She'd tried to lecture him about the women he dated, tried to suggest that he was deliberately choosing women who were career driven. Women who weren't looking for marriage and children.

That was true. So what?

It was an important part of his five-year plan. He couldn't afford to be distracted by the kind of romance his sister wanted for him. Surely she understood his perennial fear? If he took his eye off the ball, he'd make a fatal error of judgement, a bad gamble like his father's, and everything he'd tried so hard to achieve would collapse around him.

But when he'd tried to explain that to Carissa, she'd said: *I'd hate to see you take a gamble with your happiness.*

What was it with these women? Why did they think they

had a special gift of second sight that could detect happiness at twenty paces? How could Sally Finch or his sister know anything about his state of mind, his personal level of contentment?

Before Logan could get his head around this quandary, the telephone in the kitchen rang and, with an irritated sigh, he turned the music down and went to answer it.

'Hi, Logan, it's Carissa.'

Speak of the devil.

'I know you're probably terribly busy, so I won't beat about the bush. I'm ringing to ask a big favour.'

For Sally, it was business as usual at work the next morning. People who'd been at the team-building workshop smiled and greeted her. Maeve was bubbling with happiness—last night's date had been sensational.

Logan gave Sally a brief nod as he hurried past with his phone glued to his ear and then, midmorning, he completely ignored her as he hurried out again, deep in conversation with a consulting engineer. They didn't return for the rest of the day.

Sally, working hard at being sensible, decided she was pleased. Life was much easier when Logan Black didn't talk to her, didn't smile at her.

At five, she was getting ready to leave when Kim told her that some scaffolding, provided by Blackcorp, had collapsed in a big mine in Western Australia. Three men had been injured and the boss and his engineer had flown over to Perth to investigate what had gone wrong and to ensure that the injured men received the very best medical attention.

'But cheer up,' Kim said when she saw Sally's long face. 'It's not your problem and the boss is a genius at handling this kind of drama.'

'I'm sure he is.' Sally picked up her handbag, slung its strap across her shoulder. 'Actually, I think I might cheer myself up by going to see a film tonight. I need a bit of escapism.'

'I have nothing special on,' Kim said. 'Would you like company?'

Sally grinned at her. 'I'd love it.'

The boss was still away on Friday when the white roses arrived. Sally thought their ivory petals were even more perfect and fragrant than last week's blooms and, in the privacy of the lift, she buried her face in them before she delivered them to Maria Paige on the next floor.

Maria was busy on the phone so Sally put the flowers in the vase, which was once again ready and waiting. She wondered what would happen to them. Would Maria arrange for their delivery to Logan Black's lover? Would she take them home to her house? Or would they sit here, unappreciated, in this empty office for the entire weekend?

Maria remained busy so Sally left quietly, none the wiser.

Determined to use the weekend to distance herself from a certain person at work, Sally was rather pleased to see Anna and Steve that evening, even though they were only calling to drop off the children.

'Oliver's inhaler is in the bag with Rose's nappies,' said Anna, looking unusually pink-cheeked and pretty in a grey silk dress and pearls. 'He only needs it if he starts to wheeze. Two puffs should do the trick.'

Steve, whose bearlike size was accentuated by a scruffy blond beard, gave his sister a rough hug. 'Great to see you, little Sal. How are you handling the big smoke?'

'I've got it licked.' Sally grinned extra-brightly to stifle any urge of Steve's to interrogate her endlessly. He had come to her rescue that night at the dance and she needed to curb his fiercely protective instincts.

'That boss of yours has a reputation for being a tough nut to crack,' he said.

'Really?' Sally gave a carefully casual shrug. 'I'm only on the front desk, so I don't really have much to do with him.'

Fortunately, that seemed to be the right answer. Steve and Anna hurried away and Sally spent the evening reading story books aloud. Oliver didn't wheeze at all and by eight he was settled in the little back bedroom in the bed next to Rose.

Once both children were sleeping like cherubs, Sally went downstairs and read a murder mystery while flipping through television channels, struggling to stay awake until their parents returned, shortly after midnight.

The rest of the weekend, usually Sally's two favourite days of the week, seemed to stretch interminably.

Kim invited her to a friend's housewarming party on Saturday night.

'The more the merrier,' she said.

Sally knew that she needed to get out and meet young people. One of the exciting things about living in Sydney was the smorgasbord of eligible young men. Sally had hoped to meet all sorts of nice guys. But then Logan Black had fallen in a duck pond and his wet shirt and warm smiles at the team-building workshop had redefined her vision of masculinity.

How silly.

Sillier still was the fact that she couldn't dredge up enough interest in this party. Instead, she cleaned out and sorted Chloe's pantry. She visited a pet shop and thought long and hard about buying a cat for company. She went for several long walks and she sent a falsely bright and chatty email to her parents.

The boss returned to the office on Monday.

Sally looked up as the big sliding glass doors parted for a

tall, dark-suited figure and when she saw that it was Logan her heart leapt high and hard. She thought he looked strained and tired. *He definitely needs more than a cup of coffee for breakfast.*

He smiled at her—actually smiled—and said, 'Good morning, Sally.'

Sally again. Not Miss Finch, or Miss Sparrow.

'Nice to see you back,' she said as cheerfully as she could.

'Thank you, Sally. It's good to be back.'

Surprised but emboldened by his friendliness, she called after him, 'I was sorry to hear about the accident in Western Australia.'

At the security doors, Logan paused and turned back to her. 'Yes, it was bad. But the injured men are in good hands. They should make a full recovery. And we were able to put our minds at rest about our scaffolding.'

'That's good news for Blackcorp.'

He fumbled in his trouser pocket, then slanted an embarrassed smile in her direction. 'I seem to have forgotten my swipe card. Could you let me in?'

'Of course.' Sally's poor heart was close to meltdown as she pressed the buzzer on her desk to operate the security doors. They slid open with a soft swish, but Logan didn't continue through.

Instead, he stood with his hand in his trouser pocket and he stared at the foyer's marble flooring with a thoughtful frown, and the doors gently closed again. Sally was about to press the buzzer for a second time when he retraced his steps to her desk. 'Sally, I have a question.'

'Yes?' She couldn't help adding, 'I happen to know that you're rather good at asking questions.'

He responded with another small smile. 'I need a little help with something. Would it be possible for us to meet here at five this evening? I won't keep you long.'

Her mouth opened, but no sound emerged. Had she forgotten to breathe?

Logan frowned at her. 'Is that a problem?'

'Oh, no.' At last she found her voice but it was rather squeaky. 'No, it's no problem. Five o'clock is fine. Absolutely.'

'Wonderful.' He offered a brief dip of his dark head. 'I'll see you then.'

He crossed again to the security door and waited and Sally thought how totally, deliciously handsome he looked with his shiny black hair and his lovely dark eyes, his sharp white shirt and classic suit. And she knew exactly how beautiful his body was beneath that superfine clothing. Broad shoulders, deep chest, narrow hips, long powerful legs.

'Sally?' Faintly bemused, he glanced back at her. 'The door?'

'Oh, sorry.' Blushing profusely, she pressed the buzzer to let him through.

CHAPTER SIX

FORTUNATELY, it was a busy Monday morning. Sally was too occupied with telephone calls, courier deliveries, bags of mail and visitors arriving for important meetings to spend much time wondering what kind of help the boss could possibly require from her.

But the question was there, lurking in the back of her mind, along with an uneasy suspicion. Why the boss's sudden interest in her? She knew enough about human nature to understand that when someone changed from being aloof and dismissive to attentive and charming there had to be a hidden agenda.

Logan Black wanted something. From her.

But why did he need a special meeting? Why couldn't he have asked her straight out, or sent an email?

At lunch time in the park, while pigeons hovered, eyeing sandwich crusts, Sally wished she could share the boss's puzzling request with Kim. Instead, she fished for information about his white roses.

'I suppose they must be for someone special,' she suggested.

Kim pulled a face as she threw a crust that brought pigeons fluttering and swooping like paper in a whirlwind. 'I doubt it.'

'Why do you say that?'

'He seems to have a string of women. All high-flyers—

businesswomen, politicians, lawyers. Every time his photo's in the paper he's with someone different. The white roses must be for his current favourite.'

'You mean they all get the same treatment? How unimaginative!' Sally's vehemence surprised her.

Kim laughed. 'Give the man a break. He's a mere male. We can't expect too much.'

'So true,' Sally said with a sigh. But now she felt more confused than ever. At the workshop last week, when she had suggested to Logan that there was someone special in his life, he hadn't denied it. But Kim was confident that he had a procession of women.

She should be pleased about either possibility, of course. At least she now knew exactly where she stood.

Completely out of the picture.

Maria Paige rang shortly after lunch. 'Are you very busy, Sally?'

'Not especially.'

'Mr Black would like an up-to-date file of all the media coverage of Blackcorp's activities. It's a matter of searching on the Internet for articles in newspapers and mining magazines published over the last couple of months. Do you think you could manage that?'

'Sure. I can do it now if you like.'

'Wonderful. Could you make a file of the articles and then email them through to me?'

'No problem.'

As Sally turned to her computer and clicked on a search engine, she wondered if this was the 'help' Logan had wanted to discuss with her. Perhaps he'd mentioned it to Maria Paige, suggesting that it was a task suitable for Sally. Perhaps Maria had jumped in and asked Sally first to prove how super-efficient she was?

Sally was happy to do the task, but the possibility that there wouldn't be anything left to discuss with Logan at five o'clock took the shine off her afternoon.

It was interesting, however, to discover how many news stories and articles had been written about Blackcorp. By the end of the day, she had a much better grasp of the huge range of mining ventures the company supported, as well as Blackcorp's role in many industry innovations, their outstanding annual profits and the soaring value of BMC shares. It was all a little overwhelming.

Shortly before five, she sent an email with the file she'd created through to Maria, then waited nervously for the boss. He arrived at her desk at four and a half minutes past the hour.

'I hope I haven't kept you waiting.'

'No, not at all. I've just sent the media file through to Maria.'

Logan looked puzzled. 'What media file?'

'The one you wanted. The last few months' media coverage of Blackcorp.'

'Really? Maria asked *you* to compile that?'

'Yes. Was that what you planned to ask me?'

His brow furrowed as he shook his head, clearly puzzled. Then he looked at her and the frown disappeared. 'No, my question has nothing to do with work.'

'Oh.' The single syllable was almost more than Sally could manage. She stood very still, hardly daring to breathe.

Logan smiled another of his rare surprise-attack smiles. 'I'd rather not discuss it here. Do you have time for a drink? There's a quiet bar around the corner.'

Sally's sense of bewilderment deepened. This couldn't be a date, could it? Surely the boss didn't want to add her to his string of women?

Watching her, the lines at the sides of Logan's eyes crinkled. 'I promise I won't keep you long.'

'Right.' Sally gathered up her handbag and hoped he didn't notice that she was shaking. 'Let's go.'

Out on the street, the afternoon had turned gloomy and grey clouds pressed low to the tops of the city buildings. Rain threatened and the temperature had dropped and Sally hadn't brought a coat, so she was doubly glad that Logan hadn't exaggerated—the bar was, indeed, just around the corner.

Logan pushed open the gilt-framed heavy glass door and ushered Sally inside and, as the door closed behind them, the roar and beeping of peak hour traffic disappeared and they were enveloped by warmth and luxury.

The bar was unexpectedly large inside, with parquet flooring and Oriental rugs, timber panelling and plush leather armchairs. The waiters were dressed like butlers and Sally felt as if she were walking into an exclusive men's club. At first she thought all the customers were men in dark business suits, but then she realised that there were several women, also dressed in dark business suits, with serious, businesslike expressions to match.

In her pale grey suit and rose-pink top with a beaded neckline, Sally felt girlish and frivolous by comparison.

'Let's sit here,' Logan said, indicating two deep leather armchairs and a low polished table in a quiet corner. Sally sat very carefully, as she'd been taught years ago in deportment classes, knees together, feet tucked neatly, so that her legs didn't draw inappropriate attention.

A waiter approached them.

'What would you like to drink?' Logan asked her. 'Do you like wine?'

'Yes, thanks. Red or white, I don't mind.'

He ordered Cabernet Sauvignon for both of them and then, as the waiter left, he confessed, 'I know you must be wondering why on earth I've dragged you here.'

'I must admit I can't imagine why you'd need my help.'

He released a button on his jacket and let it swing open to reveal rather a lot of pale blue, very fine shirt.

Looking utterly relaxed, he said, 'My sister appealed to me to donate money to the Children's Hospital. Her husband's a doctor and she's a physiotherapist and it's a cause dear to their hearts.'

A donation to a hospital? Sally couldn't imagine where this conversation was heading.

Logan continued. 'Carissa, my sister, can be extraordinarily persuasive. She spent a few minutes talking to me about very sick children and I found myself writing a cheque with too many zeroes. But, as it turns out, I was actually buying tickets in a raffle.'

'Oh, dear.' Sally smiled and leaned forward, intrigued. 'So what did you end up with?'

'Tickets to the Hospital Ball and the honour of making a fool of myself on the dance floor with Diana Devenish.'

A ball...a dance floor... Sally's heart took off like a startled possum. *Get over it, girl, get a grip. You're not going to be there.*

She swallowed. 'Isn't Diana Devenish a television breakfast show personality?'

'The one and only.'

More calmly, she said, 'I remember reading that she won a celebrity dancing competition on television.'

'That's right.'

'And they expect you to dance with her?'

'Exactly.'

'But you can't dance. You told me last week that you're absolutely hopeless.'

The waiter chose that exact moment to arrive with their wine and Sally blushed when she realised that he must have overheard her comment. *When will I ever learn to watch what I say?*

Logan, however, looked more amused than angry and the very discreet waiter showed no sign that he'd heard her.

When they were alone again, Logan smiled and raised his glass. 'Here's to team-building.'

'To team-building.' Sally's faint response betrayed her confusion. She took a small sip of the wine, which was very dark and full-bodied and smooth. She was sure it had cost a small fortune. 'Lovely,' she said.

'It's not a bad drop.'

She still had no idea where this conversation was heading, so she set the glass down. She had to keep her wits about her.

Logan said, 'As you so rightly remembered, I'm absolutely clueless about dancing.' With a rueful smile, he took another sip of his wine.

'I don't suppose you can wriggle out of this?'

'Not without upsetting a lot of people, including my brother-in-law on the Hospital Board.'

'Well, the Children's Hospital is a very good cause,' Sally said, thinking of little Oliver and his problem with asthma. 'And I'm sure you'll be fine. No one will expect you to perform like Fred Astaire.'

Logan laughed. 'There's absolutely no chance of that.'

Sally smiled. But then she made the mistake of picturing Logan Black on a dance floor, and then, more foolishly, she imagined herself in his arms. And suddenly the bad memories were back—Kyle Francis holding her down, the smell and the taste of earth and male sweat. His hands hurting her. She felt a rush of panic and struggled to breathe as fear gripped her throat.

Fortunately, Logan didn't appear to notice her distress. 'Even without the burden of great expectations,' he said smoothly, 'I'd rather not trample all over Diana Devenish's expert toes.'

Sally nodded stiffly.

Logan's long fingers twisted the stem of his wineglass. 'I don't cherish the idea of making a complete and utter fool of myself in front of Sydney's finest.'

'You could have lessons,' Sally suggested, feeling more nervous by the second. She felt uncomfortably confused too. She still had no idea why her boss was taking her into his confidence.

Watching her, he said, 'I'll certainly need lessons. That's where you come in, Sally.'

'Me?'

'I was hoping to call on your expertise.'

'I—I don't understand.' A pulse in her throat began to beat like the wings of a trapped bird.

'When we were talking the other day, you told me that you were barely out of the cradle before you started dancing at Outback balls with all your brothers.'

'Oh—w-well, yes, that's true.'

'So I assume you're a very good ballroom dancer?'

Sally's eyes widened with shock. 'I—I'm not bad.'

'I was hoping you could teach me.'

Whack.

The impact of his words exploded inside her, shooting sparks like a firework.

'I've shocked you,' Logan said, watching her carefully.

Sally reached for her wine. 'You've certainly surprised me.' Surprised? She was fighting panic. To teach her boss to dance would be stressful enough without the horrible memories that haunted her.

'It's for a good cause,' Logan said. 'You'd be helping sick children like your nephew. The one with asthma. And many others who are much worse off. I can't imagine what it would be like to have your childhood blighted by severe illness.'

It was a very good cause. Sally couldn't deny that, but she couldn't let go of her fear at the thought of dancing. With

Logan. Her heart was racing. Her skin was bathed with perspiration and her throat had closed over.

Logan said, with a smiling shrug, 'I'd be willing to pay you, of course.'

At the mention of money, Sally blinked. *He should hire a professional.* There had to be hundreds of professional dance teachers in Sydney and Logan could hire any one of them. They would provide him with the expert coaching he needed and the added bonus of complete anonymity. And she would be spared the ordeal.

But Logan's sister might have suggested professional classes already. And, even if she hadn't, Sally knew that Logan's request was a perfect opportunity to conquer her fear once and for all.

When she was eleven she'd fallen from a horse. She'd been winded and hurt and, even now, when she thought about it, she could still remember the pain of bruised ribs and the taste of the red dust in her mouth. But, despite her skinned knees and bruises, her father had insisted that she must get straight back in the saddle.

She'd sensed then, at that tender age, that if she hadn't followed her father's advice, she might have developed a fear of horses that could have turned into a debilitating phobia.

It's the same now. I have to get back on the dance floor.

It would be silly to spend the rest of her life avoiding something she loved as much as she loved dancing. And, after all, she'd come to Sydney to prove she'd recovered from that experience.

She could almost hear her dad urging her in that gentle, insistent way of his. *Come on, kiddo. When you come a cropper, you just have to pick yourself up and ride the bruises out of your system.*

Now I need to dance the bruises out of my system.

And, of course, there was the rather astonishing fact that Logan had *asked* her.

'What are you thinking?' He looked endearingly worried.

Sally let out her breath slowly. 'I—I'm thinking that we'd need to find a suitable venue. Somewhere with space to move about.'

Relief spread over his face like a sunrise and Sally was suddenly very glad she hadn't turned him down.

'I've been giving the venue some thought,' he said. 'I wondered if the meeting room at Blackcorp would be suitable. We could push the tables and chairs against the walls.'

'I—I guess.'

'But we'd need to do this outside working hours, of course. There's no need to advertise the lessons to the staff.' He shot her a sharp questioning glance.

'I won't breathe a word,' she promised.

'I hoped an evening might be suitable. Or some time at the weekend.'

Sally nodded. 'Either time would be OK for me. I'm not especially busy.'

'How about Thursday evening, then? At about half past seven?'

Lifting her glass in a salute, Sally said, 'It's a date. I—I mean a deal. Make sure you bring your dancing shoes.'

He grinned. 'Thanks for the reminder. I might have turned up in joggers.'

'And we'll need music.'

'I'll look after that. I have a portable player. And I'll pick you up on Thursday.'

It was on the tip of Sally's tongue to tell him there was no need. She lived very close to the Glebe train station. But this man was her boss. Surely she could trust him? Besides, he drove a very sleek and expensive black car.

As she drank some more of her wine, she finally began to relax. If she stayed calm, this could actually be fun.

She said, 'You'll have to decide what styles of dance you'd like to learn. How long have we got? I doubt I could manage to teach them all.'

'Oh, no. There's no need for that. The ball's in less than a fortnight, but Diana Devenish is such an expert she can dance any style, so I just have to nominate which I'd prefer.'

'That certainly takes the pressure off. Which dance would you like to learn?'

He shrugged. 'What's the easiest?'

'It depends on your personality and your body type.' With her head to one side, Sally pretended to study her tall, dark, handsome and slightly arrogant boss. 'I don't think there's any question, actually. You should definitely choose the waltz.'

Logan's sister rang him that evening. 'I know you're going to tell me I'm a nosy sister, but I've made enquiries about ballroom dancing classes.'

'You're an exceedingly nosy sister,' he told her, without malice. 'And your efforts are appreciated, but entirely unnecessary. I've made my own arrangements.'

'For dancing classes?'

'There's no need to sound so shocked.'

'I must say I'm surprised, Logan. Very surprised. I know how you feel about dancing and I was sure you'd keep putting off classes. Who's the teacher?'

'Er—' Logan missed a beat '—a woman in Glebe.'

'Did she come highly recommended?'

He sidestepped that question. 'Relax, Carissa. I'm confident she'll be more than satisfactory.'

'Well…' Carissa was obviously struggling to take this in. 'That's…that's fantastic, little brother. Good for you.'

Logan wished, as he hung up, that he felt as certain as he'd sounded.

Now that he'd jumped in and propositioned Sally Finch he was beginning to wonder if he'd lost his grip on reality. Why, in the first place, had he confided in his newest employee about a limitation that had embarrassed him since he was a teenager? And why had he then gone one step further and asked her to help him overcome that handicap?

The rushed trip to Western Australia must have taken its toll and left him with weakened defences. What other explanation could there be? He'd walked through Blackcorp's doors this morning, had taken one look at Sally and his common sense had melted like cheap plastic in a microwave.

Then again, he argued a moment later, why not hire Sally's expertise? His knowledge of dance teachers was severely limited, but he was sure she had the necessary credentials—a slim build, energy and grace. Good communication skills.

Logan's alternative was a professional teacher and he didn't fancy being bossed around by an indifferent stranger who dealt with an endless stream of enthusiastic pupils.

Sally was a sensitive, feeling type—Janet Keaton had said so—and she would understand how uneasy he felt about dancing. Better still, she was an employee, so he'd still have the upper hand. Of course, he would pay her well for her trouble.

Everything would be fine as long as he made sure that the lessons didn't upset their boss-employee dynamics.

That settled, Logan's conscience was clear. Once this waltzing distraction had been discreetly and efficiently dealt with, he would be able to get straight back to his far more important responsibilities and focus one hundred per cent on his business.

Sally floated in a muddled daze through the next few days. At work she was grateful for the many distractions and at home she gave herself a thousand lectures. It was vitally important that she didn't read too much into the boss's request for dancing lessons. It was simply a logical extension of their conversation at the team-building workshop.

She was sure that the boss of Blackcorp had no hidden romantic agenda and she had to stop magnifying the significance of their rendezvous in the wine bar, had to stop reliving the utterly divine experience of sitting beside him in his luxurious car as he'd driven her home. And she mustn't dwell on how charmingly he'd chatted, offering fascinating insights into places of interest around Sydney.

There was no way the lessons would lead to anything romantic. It was out of the question. Just imagine, an affair between the boss and his most lowly employee. What a joke. She was a girl from the bush and she didn't fit into his city scene at all.

And the last thing she wanted was to join the long list of women who'd received his weekly offering of roses. Actually, Sally couldn't help wondering, why hadn't Logan asked one of them to teach him to dance? Was it beneath these high-flyers' dignity? Or was it simply that Logan wanted to keep this one little inadequacy a secret from the rest of the world?

Whatever her boss's reason for seeking her out, one thing was certain: when the dance class started, their roles would be reversed. She would be the one with the expertise. She would be the teacher and Logan Black would be the pupil.

In charge of the boss. It was a mind-twisting thought.

CHAPTER SEVEN

THURSDAY evening began with Logan's arrival on Sally's doorstep, which was an event in itself. He was wearing battered jeans and a faded blue T-shirt, thin from much washing, and when Sally opened her door she forgot that it was rude to stare.

He looked so different! So casual and relaxed and—*gulp*—even more drop-dead divine than usual.

'Is something wrong?' he asked.

'No, nothing's wrong,' Sally squeaked. 'Nothing at all.'

He pointed to his feet. 'I remembered the shoes.'

Dragging her gaze reluctantly downwards, she saw that he was indeed wearing his leather lace-ups. 'Well done.'

For most of the short journey through the dark city streets, she tried to put into practice what she'd learned at yoga classes about keeping calm and balanced. *It's all in the breathing. Keep your breaths even and steady. In, two, three, four, five, six, seven, eight. Out, two, three, four, five, six, seven, eight.*

Fortunately, Logan was happy to concentrate on the traffic and he didn't try to distract her with scintillating conversation. There was no way Sally could calm down and scintillate at the same time.

They reached the underground car park beneath Blackcorp's offices and parked in the space assigned to BMC's Managing

Director. The lighting was minimal and their footsteps echoed eerily in the empty subterranean chamber as they made their way to the lift.

Sally's heartbeat raced and she felt wings of panic, but soon they were inside the main building and the security guy bustled up to them importantly as Logan was unlocking Blackcorp's door.

'Everything all right, Mr Black?' His eyes bulged with curiosity when he saw Sally.

'Of course, Reg. Perfectly fine.' If Logan was embarrassed to be caught after hours, sneaking back into the office with the front desk girl, he hid the fact behind a ferocious frown. 'Miss Finch and I are working on a special project.'

'Oh, right then, sir. I'll leave you to it.'

Sally was relieved to know that the guard was close by as she and Logan went through both sets of doors, then along the hall to the meeting room. They became very efficient as they pushed tables and chairs to the sides to make a space in the centre. Logan set up his portable player and switched it on and the bright notes of a Strauss waltz filled the room.

'Will this music be OK?' he asked.

Sally wrinkled her nose. 'It might be a bit old-fashioned for a modern ball, but it's the real thing!'

'Everything's ready, then.' He stood to attention and took a deep breath. 'Now, what do I have to do?'

Looking at him as he stood there, his expression so tense and serious, Sally's nervousness evaporated. Logan Black wasn't the rat who'd been so vile at the country dance. Right now, he was barely recognisable as her arrogant and distant boss.

He was a vulnerable man who would be mortified if his inadequacies were exposed, and yet, conscientious to a fault, he was determined to do the right thing by his sister.

He genuinely needed her help.

Smiling her warmest smile, Sally walked towards him, reached for his hands and took them lightly in hers. The tentative contact was enough to launch her into orbit, but she schooled herself to ignore the sizzle and to concentrate on helping him to waltz.

She was determined to do her absolute best.

This was a bad idea. A very bad idea.

The instant Sally's warm hands clasped his, Logan knew he was in trouble.

To start with, Sally was wearing a sleeveless yellow dress made from some kind of T-shirt material. With a low-backed top that hugged her lithe body like a leotard and a full skirt that rippled about her legs whenever she moved, the outfit was no doubt very suitable for dancing. But it totally threatened the boss-employee dynamics he'd been determined to maintain.

And now she was standing close and touching him. Her bright hair framed her intent face, her eyes signalled intelligence and sensitivity, and all he wanted to do was haul her closer and kiss her and—

'The waltz is all about poise, grace and elegance,' she told him. 'If you listen carefully to the music, you can hear how light and smooth and airy it is.'

Obediently, Logan censored his thoughts and concentrated on Strauss's *Blue Danube*. 'The beat's important, isn't it?'

'Absolutely. Counting the music is most important. That's what will get you through this waltz. Can you count to three, Mr Black?'

He favoured her with a lopsided smile.

'Oh, yes, of course,' Sally said in mock apology. 'You've already told me you're very good at mathematics, so this should be a cinch.'

He couldn't help admiring her confidence and her easy use of humour to help him to relax. She really was a surprise package—and, right now, very much in control.

'All you have to do is count to three,' she continued. '*One* is the most important. You need to emphasise the first beat.'

Holding his left hand in her right, she beat in time to the music. 'Hear it? *One*, two, three. *One*, two, three. *One*, two, three.'

'Yep. Got that.'

'The other key to the waltz is posture.'

Automatically, Logan thrust his jaw forward and his shoulders back.

'Not like that. We don't want you standing like a wooden soldier. You need to be lifted and light on your feet. You mustn't weigh your partner down.' Her eyes twinkled at him. 'On the dance floor, the man becomes his partner's coat hanger.'

'That's a role I've never aspired to.'

'It's important to remember,' she said, suppressing a smile. 'You need to be strong and supportive, so your arms can provide the frame for Diana Devenish to look fabulous.'

'Right.' Logan turned his grimace into a smile. 'An awesome responsibility.'

'You'll be fine, Logan,' she said more gently.

Logan.

It was the first time Sally had used his first name and it bothered him that he'd noticed. Why? It was of no particular significance, but simply part of her technique to get him to relax.

And yet, somehow, crazily, it felt like a big deal.

'Now,' she said, 'place your right hand just below my scapula.'

'Your what?'

'Sorry. Too many first aid classes. Put your hand just below my shoulder blade.'

Her shoulder blade...

Valiantly, Logan attempted to follow her instruction but, as soon as his fingers made contact with her soft, exposed skin, he inhaled sharply and retracted his hand abruptly.

She had to be joking.

He shifted his hand lower to the safety of clothing. *The further away from her bare skin the better.*

'Not my waist, my shoulder blade.' Reaching behind, Sally slid his hand up her back. 'Just think bra line.' Her eyes narrowed shrewdly and she looked at him with a cheeky tilt of her head. 'I'm quite sure you've managed to find *that* on a woman before.'

Very true. So why was he breaking out in a cold sweat now?

'Now, let's count to three and—' Frowning at him, Sally hesitated. 'Are you OK?'

'Never better,' he lied. With his hand at Sally's bra line, counting to three was suddenly as easy as climbing Mount Everest with frostbite.

'Fabulous. Now, we'll step out the beat. Let's go. One, two, three. One, two, three. Left, right, left. Right, left, right.'

Somehow, Logan managed to survive this without trampling on Sally's toes and they actually completed a circuit around the cleared floor.

'You make it easy,' he told her somewhat triumphantly.

'You're doing really well, but we've a little way to go yet. Now, I want you to make the first beat strong and the second two lighter. Strong, soft, soft. Strong, soft, soft.'

They whirled together, bumped knees once or twice, but continued on without any major mishap.

'Great!' Sally cried. 'Now you're really getting it!'

He could have kissed her—*might* have kissed her—but she was too busy issuing more instructions.

'OK. Now you still need to emphasise the first beat, but

I'd like you to make the steps a bit oozy. Kind of like sliding in syrup.'

'In syrup?' he echoed faintly.

'Mmm. You need to keep in time, but try changing the quality to a smooth, gentle, gliding motion.'

Sally demonstrated, moving away from him, gliding smoothly, fluid as air.

'I'll never be able to do that.'

'Don't be defeatist,' she scolded.

'I'm a realist.'

But it seemed that Sally had no plans to give up on him.

'Let's look at this another way, then.' Tapping a finger against her lips, she watched him thoughtfully. 'Let me see. You're a wine connoisseur. Why don't you think of the waltz as a fine red?'

His eyebrows arched with bemusement. 'How is that supposed to help?'

'Imagine Diana Devenish as some kind of exquisite Cabernet Sauvignon—rich and complex, yet mysterious. You give her a swirl and admire her finer qualities, including her fabulous legs, and all the while you're careful not to spill a drop. You take the wine slowly, savouring every sip as it glides smoothly down your throat. Except you're gliding along the dance floor instead!'

Logan grinned. 'That kind of works for me. I'll give it a go.'

Once again, she stepped towards him, took his hand and assumed the dancing position. Taking a deep breath, he placed his hand at her bra line and tried to ignore her tantalising, silky-soft skin. Sally was amazing. Fancy likening the waltz to wine. But it worked. He could picture it. How many intriguing layers were there to this girl?

'OK, let's glide, Logan.'

Drawing Sally in, Logan glided. One, two, three. Strong,

soft, soft. She was light and graceful in his arms and, as they whirled, he caught wafts of her enticing, tormenting perfume. And somewhere, in the midst of it all, he gave up worrying and let go, giving in, at last, to the moment, to the flow of the music.

Sally was probably right. Dancing was like drinking fine wine. He certainly longed to know how *she* tasted, couldn't shake the feeling that she would be one of those rare finds, imparting a surprisingly delicious aftertaste that left him wanting more.

Yes, he definitely wanted more, wanted Sally's slender curves pressed more closely against him, wanted her soft lips—

Logan stumbled. 'I'm so sorry.'

In the next breath he realised that his stumble hadn't been caused by his own inadequacies, but by Sally, who had stopped dancing and was now slipping out of his arms.

Flushed and trembling, she stood with her hands buried in the folds of her skirt, not looking at him.

'That—that was very good,' she said. 'You're really getting the hang of it.'

'You're a very good teacher,' he assured her and he might have added more compliments but, watching her intently, he realised that something was wrong. Very wrong.

How had this sudden change happened? Why? Had he held her too tightly? God forbid she'd sensed the direction of his thoughts.

She still wouldn't look at him and she had completely lost her sparkle. Clouds had arrived to cover the stars.

'That's probably enough for one night,' she said.

What could he do but agree?

'Thank you,' he said quietly. 'I really appreciate your help.'

One corner of her mouth lifted into a sadly wry smile, then she turned and crossed the room and switched off the music and the silence seemed to echo in the big empty room.

'And now I must pay you,' Logan said.

'Oh, no.' Sally's hands rose to stop him. 'There's no need. I'm happy to do this—but I'm not a professional.'

He cursed himself for handling this so clumsily. 'I'm going to need more tuition before the ball.'

She nodded unhappily.

'Perhaps I could take you to dinner in lieu of payment.' It was an idea that had just come to him and he couldn't imagine why he hadn't thought of it sooner. 'After all, you'll be giving up your evenings.'

Eyes fixed on her clasped hands, Sally continued to look unhappy. 'I don't think dinner's a good idea.'

'Why ever not?'

She looked up then and her blue eyes shone with an unnatural intensity. 'It would be too much like a date.'

'And that's a crime?'

'You're my boss, remember?'

'Well, yes. That's…true.' Logan scratched his jaw. Somehow, his original plan to keep business and pleasure apart no longer made any sense. He was quite sure that he and Sally should have dinner together. The sooner the better. 'Let's keep Blackcorp out of this. You'll be sacrificing your evenings to help me. Surely I owe you one dinner.'

Chin lifted, Sally answered him with a long and challenging stare. 'Isn't there someone who might object if we had dinner together?'

'I can't think of anyone.'

Her eyes widened. 'What about the white roses women?'

'The *who*?'

She gave an impatient toss of her lively curls and glared at him. 'Don't play dumb, Mr Black. You know very well who I'm talking about. You have a standing order for white roses and they come every Friday and they're always for a woman, aren't they?'

'Well...yes,' he admitted, admiring her spirit. 'You're absolutely right. The roses are most definitely for a woman.'

Sally blinked hard and looked away. 'Does she know you're having dancing lessons with me?'

'No. She has no idea.'

'Are you planning to inform her that you've invited me to dinner?'

'I must admit I haven't given it any thought, but I don't see why I couldn't tell her.'

In the face of his calm responses, Sally's self-righteous certainty lost a little of its starch. She cast an anxious glance about the meeting room, then lifted her shoulders in an annoyed shrug. 'We'd better get this place tidied up.'

'There's no need. The cleaners will appreciate having a cleared floor to work with and they'll rearrange the furniture in the morning.'

'Fine.' Mouth tightly pursed, Sally unplugged Logan's player and wound the cord rapidly and neatly.

'Thank you,' he said as she handed it to him. 'Now, about dinner.'

To his dismay, Sally closed her eyes as if the very idea of dinner with him was upsetting.

Unwilling to be put off, he said quickly, 'You're right. I should clear this with the white roses woman, as you call her.'

Her blue eyes flew open.

'Why don't you come with me to meet her, Sally?'

Her jaw sagged and Logan watched the play of emotions on her expressive face as her anger morphed into doubt and confusion.

He pressed his advantage. 'We can kill two birds with one stone. You can make sure that our dinner is not interpreted as a date. And she'll enjoy meeting you very much.'

'Do you really think so?'

'I'm sure of it.'

Sally let this sink in. After a bit, she said, 'I would certainly be much happier if everything was out in the open. Where I come from, I'm used to people being up front and honest and I'd hate to go behind another woman's back.'

'That's very commendable,' Logan agreed with necessary gravity. 'Why don't you come with me tomorrow when I deliver the roses? We'll clear the air and then we can have dinner.'

It seemed an age that she stood there, considering this. He held his breath, bracing himself for her refusal, but then she shrugged. 'That seems reasonable.'

CHAPTER EIGHT

SALLY tried to carry on at work as if nothing in her life had changed, but it was a tall order considering that everything had changed while she'd been dancing with Logan Black.

To start with she'd discovered she'd fallen helplessly in love with him, which was a whopping big problem on its own. But then he'd made everything worse by moving in close to her. She'd felt his body heat and every inch of her skin had tightened…

Tingled…

Yearned…

It could have been a delicious moment, *might* have *become* a delicious moment, if her mind hadn't flashed to that other time. That other dancing partner.

Instead of bliss, panic had flared without warning.

The only good thing was that she hadn't dissolved into a quivering, gibbering mess. She'd been pleased, actually, that she'd managed to recover fairly quickly. But then Logan had complicated everything again by asking her out to dinner.

He'd made it sound so simple and straightforward—nothing more than payment for the lessons. But any way Sally looked at dinner with Logan Black it was complex, thorny, problematical…

To start with, every girl knew that dating the boss was a lightning-rod for trouble. If the rest of the staff found out, they would immediately conclude she was hungry for a fast-tracked promotion. And if office gossip wasn't something huge to fret about, there was the whole business of the white roses.

Talk about confusing. Sally suspected that very few women—even women as sophisticated as Chloe had been—had the savoir faire to meet their boss's current lover and then head off to dinner with him.

But Logan had assured her there'd be no problem and, in the end, his unruffled certainty had tipped the balance. It was why she'd said yes.

After all, he stood to lose more than she did if news of their dinner date became water-cooler gossip at Blackcorp. And it was *his* problem if their dinner upset his lover. If he could be calm about that, why shouldn't she?

Nevertheless, whenever Sally thought about that evening, she discovered it was possible to look forward to a date and dread it at the same time.

Not surprisingly, when Logan arrived at her house at six-thirty her stomach was a mass of nerves. He'd quickly showered and changed, as she had, and now he was wearing casual beige trousers and a dark shirt beneath a rather sporty lightweight jacket.

His hair was still damp and Sally, in her best little black dress and kitten heels—because there was no point in *not* looking her best—could smell his aftershave as he opened the car door for her. Once inside the car, she smelled the scent of the white roses, which were glistening on the back seat, and her stomach tightened.

Logan tried to make conversation as he drove to Clifton House, but for once Sally was too tense to respond with anything more than monosyllables. Eventually he gave up and the journey was completed in uncomfortable silence.

They arrived at very large iron gates, which were opened by a man in a little sentry box. The man greeted Logan and actually dipped his cap as the black car purred through the gateway and up a long gravelled drive that wound its way through green parkland.

Sally gasped. 'Where is this? It looks like the grounds of a mansion.'

'Clifton House,' was Logan's brief and unsatisfactory reply.

They emerged from a grove of trees into a wide courtyard complete with a beautiful fountain. In the rays of the setting sun, two storeys of windows glinted gold. This *was* a mansion. And Sally was way, way out of her comfort zone.

The name—Clifton House—had been embellished in gold on a black sign. And then, beneath it in smaller print, were the words *Nursing Home*.

Sally rounded on Logan. 'I don't understand.'

As he steered his car into a parking space between graceful sandstone columns, he shot her a sheepish smile. 'This is where I bring the white roses.'

'Is—is the woman you love sick? Or does she run this place?'

'Her health is quite delicate.'

'What does that mean? Has she been seriously ill? Or through some kind of detox programme?'

'God forbid.'

Slipping out of his seat, he opened the rear door and retrieved the roses and then he came around to open Sally's door, but she beat him to it. 'What's going on, Logan? This isn't making sense.'

He grinned. 'Just be patient and all will be revealed.'

Stamping her foot angrily, Sally fumed. 'I'm not setting foot inside this place until I know who I'm supposed to be meeting.'

She stamped her foot again. 'And why she's in a nursing home. And why you've got such a silly grin on your face.'

'Bravo!' cried a voice from behind her.

Spinning round, Sally discovered a diminutive old lady in a motorised wheelchair. The woman's face was a picture of delighted surprise and her lively brown eyes twinkled from beneath a tidy cap of snowy curls.

'I like to see a young woman with fire,' she said.

'Darling,' Logan intervened, stooping quickly to kiss the old lady's papery cheek and settling the bouquet of roses gently in her lap, 'what are you doing outside at this hour?'

'It's such a lovely evening, I thought I'd come out to meet you. And I'm very glad I did. Now, introduce me to this interesting young woman.'

There was a flash of emotion in Logan's eyes that Sally couldn't quite identify. It was followed by a charming smile of apology. 'Grandmother, this is Sally Finch.'

Why hadn't she guessed that the white roses were for someone like a grandmother? Why hadn't Maeve or Kim guessed? The nerve of Logan to let his staff think they were for his lover!

'Sally,' Logan continued, 'I'd like you to meet my wonderful and formidable grandmother, Hattie Lane.'

Swallowing her outrage, Sally dredged up a smile as she offered her hand to be clasped by thin and wrinkled fingers. 'Pleased to meet you, Mrs Lane.'

'I'm very pleased to meet you, Sally, and please call me Hattie.'

'Now,' Logan said quickly, ignoring his grandmother's sharp, birdlike glances of bristling curiosity, 'let's get you inside, out of this night air.'

Taking hold of her wheelchair, he propelled it towards the front doorway.

Clifton House was certainly fancier than any nursing home

Sally had visited, more like a grand hotel. Logan's grandmother's room was on the ground floor. Spacious and airy, it housed a large bed with a beautiful quilted cream bedspread, built-in bookshelves and an *en suite* bathroom. There was also a small sitting area with armchairs and a coffee table beside tall French windows that opened out to the garden.

'Take a seat, Sally.' Hattie Lane, as regal in her wheelchair as on a throne, pointed to an armchair deeply upholstered in pale green velvet. 'That chair next to the window is very comfortable.'

Sally sat where she was told and watched with mild surprise as Logan arranged the bouquet of white roses in a beautiful pink crystal vase. His long fingers worked deftly and the results were surprisingly pleasing to the eye.

'Thank you, darling.' His grandmother smiled at him fondly, then, with an extra twinkle in her eyes, she asked, 'And now, how about pouring us a little sherry?'

Obediently, Logan went to a pretty cupboard in the corner and extracted three fragile gold-rimmed sherry glasses and a matching carafe with a heavy glass stopper.

'This must be a special occasion,' he said.

'Of course it's a special occasion. It's the first time you've ever brought one of your young lady friends to visit me.'

Sally wished she hadn't been looking at Logan then, hadn't seen his frown and the sudden tightening of his mouth. Clearly, he wasn't pleased that his grandmother had jumped to incorrect conclusions about their relationship.

Serves him right for tricking me into coming here.

If she'd had time, Sally might have asked herself why Logan had brought her here, but right now she decided it was more important to set the record straight with Hattie and to make sure she understood that Sally wasn't one of her grandson's 'young lady friends'.

Too nervous to take time to find a delicate way of putting

this, Sally blurted out quickly, 'I'm not actually Logan's girlfriend. I work at Blackcorp, you see. I started there a couple of weeks ago as a receptionist, but then Mr Black needed dancing lessons and I've been helping him.'

Sally felt better now that she'd got that out, but Hattie's air of excitement hadn't dimmed one jot.

'How interesting,' she said and she beamed at her grandson. 'So you're finally learning to dance, Logan.'

He tried to shrug this aside. 'It's all Carissa's doing. She talked me into a charity do at the Hospital Ball, even though she knows I can't dance to save myself.'

'But he's learning fast,' Sally told her.

'I'm sure the dear boy's a very fast learner.' Hattie made no attempt to hide her delighted amusement.

Still flustered, Sally said, 'And…and he's taking me to dinner tonight, but it…it's only a kind of thank you.'

Hattie actually laughed. 'What an excellent idea!'

Worried that Logan's grandmother might still have the wrong end of the stick, Sally considered further explanation, but Logan thrust a glass of sherry into her hand.

'Why don't we drink to my grandmother's health?' He spoke smoothly, but his eyes signalled a clear warning that Sally had said quite enough.

Lifting his glass, he said to Hattie, 'Here's to your good health, old girl.'

'Your good health,' echoed Sally.

'And yours, darlings.' Hattie beamed at them both as if they were very good children who had pleased her greatly.

Unused to such sweet fortified wine, Sally sipped carefully.

Hattie downed a hefty swig, then waved her glass in the direction of the roses. 'Aren't these blooms lovely, Sally?'

'Gorgeous.'

'Did you know Logan brings them to me every week?'

Sally squashed her urge to explain that she'd been mightily deceived about those roses. 'How kind,' she said instead.

'It's very extravagant of him, the naughty boy. Some weeks I pass on perfectly good roses to my friends. They're very happy to take them, of course.'

Leaning closer, Hattie actually winked at Sally. 'I used to grow white Bianca roses like these when Logan and his sister were children. Logan used to love playing in my garden, so the roses bring back happy memories for both of us.'

For a moment Sally was lost in a picture of Logan as a black-haired little boy, playing in a garden with grubby knees and a torn T-shirt, letting out blood-curdling yells as he threw himself into the same rough-and-tumble games her brothers had loved.

And now here he was, all grown up and successful and bringing roses to his grandmother every week. She wondered what everyone at Blackcorp would think if they knew their serious and career-oriented boss had such a kind streak.

How many men would bother?

Sally realised that Hattie's gaze was fixed on her, watching her face intently, and she hoped she hadn't been looking too wistful. Smiling quickly, she struggled to think of a way to change the subject and remembered what Logan had told her at the team-building workshop. 'Am I right in believing that you used to be a concert pianist, Hattie?'

'I was indeed.' Hattie looked down at her knuckles gnarled with age and her fingers knotted with arthritis. 'How I loved my piano. But I can barely knock out a tune now.'

'Sally's a fan of Brahms,' Logan said.

'Are you really, dear?'

His grandmother's instant pleasure made Sally squirm. She wasn't at all sure that liking one piece of music by a particular composer elevated her to fandom.

'I…I don't know very much about classical music.'

'That doesn't matter. Logan will teach you,' Hattie pronounced with blithe confidence. 'It's a fair exchange, isn't it? My grandson can teach you about music and you can teach him to dance.'

'That was unfair,' Sally remarked as Logan drove back into the city, late for their dinner engagement because she and Hattie had spent such a long time chatting. 'You should have warned me that the roses were for your sweet little grandmother.'

In the glare of the oncoming headlights, Logan saw her indignant frown and braced himself for the attack he knew he deserved.

'Why have you let everyone in the office think the roses were for your lovers?'

'Is that what everyone thinks?'

'Most,' Sally amended hotly.

'I'm afraid they overestimate me, Sally. I'm not given to daft romantic gestures. The women I date never expect anything like that.'

Sally opened her mouth. Shut it again, then frowned. Unhappily, she said, 'But you let the rumour spread.'

'Look, Sally, for a start, a boss shouldn't get involved in office gossip.' He chanced a smile. 'Secondly, why spoil a good story with the truth? More importantly, Hattie is family. She's none of Blackcorp's business.'

'So why did you take me to see her?'

It was a very fair question. Logan wished he could offer a definitive answer. His decision had felt instinctive, but he'd never been an intuitive type, so taking Sally to visit his grandmother on a whim had been completely out of character.

Almost everything he'd done since he met Sally was out of

character. He would have to rectify that. Very soon. But right now he could think of no plausible explanation to offer her except the simple truth. 'I knew you two would get on well.'

Sally considered this and said after a bit, 'OK, maybe you were right about us hitting it off. Hattie's an absolute darling. But if you've never taken any of your…um…female friends to see her before, aren't you worried that she might read deeper significance into my visit?'

With the twenty-twenty vision of hindsight, Logan had to agree. He'd taken one look at Hattie's animated delight and he'd known that his impulse to bring Sally was foolish. But their dancing class had cast some kind of spell on him and the impulsive invitation had made perfect sense at the time.

Later, he'd been attacked by doubts, but then he'd applied logic and had come up with the same answer. Sally Finch got on well with everyone. With her gift for making friends, she would brighten his grandmother's life and give the poor old girl the lift she needed.

It wasn't much fun for an intelligent, lively woman who'd had a passion for life and a brilliant artistic career to end up in a nursing home. But Hattie couldn't live alone any more and she couldn't stay with Logan's parents. She'd never got on with his father. And she hadn't wanted to impose herself on either Logan or Carissa.

Now his parents were travelling around Australia in their caravan—doing the lap of honour, as his mother called it. Carissa was busy with her career and her family and Logan had assumed the responsibility of keeping an eye on Hattie.

Until tonight, he'd always visited her alone. So taking Sally had been something of a risk. Crazy, no doubt.

In the car's darkened interior, he sent her a repentant smile. 'You deserve an apology. I'm sorry. My bad joke misfired. I should have explained about Hattie.'

'I'm just embarrassed that she assumes we're a couple.'

'I'll resolve that confusion next time I see her.'

If Logan expected this to soothe Sally, he was out of luck. With a little huff of annoyance, she crossed her arms and then her legs and sat very stiffly, staring away from him through the passenger window.

The view of her legs, revealed by a short black skirt and encased in sheer tights, became a traffic hazard and he manfully kept his attention on the road.

He had reserved a table at his favourite restaurant, nestled close to the water in a cove of Sydney Harbour. As always, he was greeted like an old friend by Marco, the head waiter, who didn't mind at all that he and Sally were late. He showed them to their table, set by a huge window.

It was a rare pleasure to watch the delight in Sally's face when she saw the view of the water and sparkling reflections, the lights of the harbour bridge and the city beyond.

Marco seemed to enjoy watching her too and, as he whisked out her table napkin and set it on her lap, he sent Logan a silent, wide-eyed, *Wow!*

Logan had to remind himself that this wasn't a real date. He was only bringing Sally here because he owed her for the lessons.

It helped to remember that Sally wasn't his type. She was warm and generous and lovely—distractingly lovely tonight in her little black dress—but she was also an idealist and a hopeless romantic.

Until he'd achieved his long-term business goals, he simply couldn't afford to become entangled with a girl like her. Tonight, he would be polite and distant, offering courtesy and friendliness, but extra careful to keep everything on a strictly business level.

'This is a gorgeous restaurant.' Sally smiled her approval

as she took in details of the clean and restrained décor, the crisp white tablecloths, the pale timber floors and modern lighting.

'The chef here is superb,' he told her, sending a salute to the busy open-plan kitchen. 'He's French, but the menu is very cosmopolitan and there's always a good selection.'

Sally studied the menu carefully and her brow furrowed more deeply as she progressed.

Logan wondered what was wrong. Carefully, he asked, 'Does anything there take your fancy?'

'It all sounds lovely, but everything's so expensive. The fee for one dancing class might buy me a bowl of soup, but not much more.'

Good grief. Was she serious?

He caught a wicked gleam in the china-blue eyes watching him over the menu and knew she was teasing, was surprised by how much this delighted him.

'Let me see,' he said, poker-faced. 'I'd estimate that this dinner should cover the cost of one, maybe two lessons.'

Lowering her gaze to the menu, Sally replied serenely, 'But we'd better not have wine. That would push the price way too high.'

'Unless you escorted me to the ball as well.'

The menu slipped from Sally's hands as quickly as the colour left her cheeks. 'You can't mean that.'

She was right. Logan couldn't believe he'd made such a reckless suggestion. He was never impulsive!

'Look,' he said, exasperated by his inability to remain sensible and composed in this woman's presence, 'let's forget about the ball for now. It's Friday evening and it's getting late and we're hungry. I'd like to enjoy a pleasant meal and I've invited you to share it with me. Let's leave it at that.'

'Right,' Sally said with surprising meekness.

He thought he'd dampened her spirits then, so he was

relieved that they enjoyed a very pleasant evening. The meal began with an excellent vichyssoise soup, followed by a schnitzel pan fried with parmesan for Sally, who thought it was 'fabulous', while Logan had a superb Greek lamb dish. For dessert he chose a chocolate pot and Sally a light lemon tart.

While they ate, they talked sensibly about places they'd visited, books they'd read and movies they'd seen. Logan found himself laughing at some of Sally's witty observations and there were times when he had to remember to stop smiling. But for the most part they shared a safe and impersonal conversation. He thanked heavens that Sally had got the message that this was payment and not a date.

The only hiccup arrived with their coffee, when the dashing French chef, Michel, brought an extra coffee cup and joined them at their table.

Michel was an old friend of Logan's and he'd developed a ritual of sharing coffee with him towards the end of the evening, when the pace in the kitchen slowed and could be dealt with by minions. Logan usually enjoyed his friend's company.

But tonight, Michel, with his Frenchman's love of romance, took a long look at Sally and Logan knew there'd be trouble.

The chef's dark eyes flashed a thousand fervent signals as he bent low to kiss Sally's hand. 'Enchanted to meet you, *mademoiselle*,' he murmured in his sexiest accent.

Sally was incredibly flattered, of course, and Logan struggled with a ridiculous urge to tell his good friend to get lost.

'You're a sensational chef,' Sally told Michel. 'The food tonight was divine.'

Michel pressed a melodramatic hand to his heart. 'My constant inspiration is the knowledge that a beautiful woman like you will be eating my food.'

Sally laughed and then she shot Logan a telling glance. 'I guess you must come here often.'

'My friend has superb taste,' Michel said, giving Logan's shoulder an enthusiastic thump.

'And I dare say he provides you with lots of inspiration,' Sally suggested silkily, 'via his companions.'

There was a mischievous glint in Sally's eyes, but Logan glared at her.

Michel guffawed and clapped his hands. 'Ah, but tonight my good friend has surpassed himself.'

'Be careful, Michel.' Logan was compelled to set the record straight. 'Sally is a colleague and tonight's dinner is a—a business dinner.'

Throwing up his hands in horror, Michel cried, 'A business dinner on a Friday night? What a terrible thought. Logan, I thought you were much more sensitive than that.'

Despite his discomfort, Logan managed to grin. 'OK, mate, I won't insult you. It's impossible to discuss business with such amazing food as yours.'

'So, Sall*ee*,' Michel said, adding charming emphasis to the second syllable, 'what do you think? Was your mind totally focused on business tonight? Or were you swept away by my brilliance in the kitchen?'

'Oh, from the moment I stepped through the door, I was totally, *totally* swept away.'

'Yes, yes!' Michel grinned widely and leapt to his feet. 'You see, Logan. This wonderful woman, she understands. And I was watching from the kitchen, you know.' He tapped the side of his arrogant French nose with a long forefinger and grinned. 'We all know that this was no business dinner.'

If Michel saw Logan's gritted teeth and clenched jaw, he made no sign, but perhaps the chef knew he'd played this to the hilt and that it was time to depart. Taking Sally's hand, he kissed it once more, gave Logan a parting salute, then abruptly returned to his kitchen.

'Bit over the top, wasn't he?' Logan muttered when they were alone once more.

'I guess he's allowed to be when he produces such fabulous food.'

'I thought you might have been embarrassed that yet another person latched on to the wrong idea about us. It's annoying when we've both been clear from the start that this wasn't a date.'

She didn't meet his gaze, gave a small shrug. 'I don't think we've done anything or said anything tonight that crossed the line between a business arrangement and a date, do you?'

'No, no, of course not.'

Eyes still lowered, Sally fiddled with the napkin on her lap.

Anxious that the evening didn't end on a bad note, Logan tried to make amends. 'It's all a game with Michel. He's French and he's a hopeless romantic. He likes to think his little restaurant can turn total strangers into lovers at one sitting.'

Sally offered a tiny smile. 'Don't worry. I was joking about being carried away. I know very well that it takes more than a dinner date for two people to fall in love.'

Logan was sure that this comment should have given him comfort, but was dismayed that he felt even worse.

CHAPTER NINE

OUTSIDE the restaurant, a chilling breeze whipped at Sally's hair and she wished she felt happier after such a magical evening. She'd adored every moment of Logan's company, and she'd watched him relax, had seen the way his gorgeous smile lingered more and more often, had seen the glow in his eyes when he'd looked at her.

It had seemed such a fitting sequel to earlier this evening, when Logan had taken her to meet Hattie and he'd shown her the softer side she'd always suspected. Better still, he hadn't tried to hide his pleasure that his grandmother liked Sally. And now it appeared that he wasn't in a serious relationship with another woman.

Barriers had been tumbling left and right and, at some deeply intuitive level, Sally had sensed that this evening had been special for both of them. No matter how loudly they tried to deny it, strong threads of attraction had been drawing them closer and closer.

But at the end, with the chef's arrival, the delicate balance had been upset. It was as if she'd been weaving a wonderful fiction, but had suddenly been forced to face bald facts. *Wake up, Sally Finch! Tonight has been a fairy tale. The boss and his front desk girl are not going to have a meaningful romance.*

Now, as the lights of the restaurant narrowed to yellow dots in the distance, the truth of her situation became plainer to Sally. She'd finally become relaxed and confident around her boss, but somehow, in the process, she'd forgotten that he was unattainable. She was playing out of her league.

The annoying thing was that deep down she *had* known that. She and Logan were poles apart and a country bumpkin, newly arrived in the big smoke, could not expect to capture the heart of a high-flying corporate executive. Sydney was overflowing with women who operated on Logan's wavelength, business and professional women with a great deal more to offer a man than mere chatting and dancing skills.

Sally had no chance of competing. It would take years and years of city life before she developed the finely honed sophistication and fashion know-how of the women who'd been born and bred here.

So what if Logan had been relaxed and happy this evening? Dinner and pleasant conversation did not mean that she and the boss were an item.

Now, as they walked beside the harbour to the parked car, their tense silence seemed to magnify the sounds of the night. Footsteps on paving stones. Waves from the wake of a boat slap-slapping against the harbour's rock wall. The blast of a ferry's horn, warning that it was about to leave Circular Quay.

A fresh burst of wind gusted across the inky water, making Sally shiver.

'You're cold,' Logan said. 'Here, have my jacket.' Gallantly, he ignored her protests that it wasn't far to the car and he slipped his jacket around her shoulders.

'Thanks,' she whispered and a high voltage thrill zapped through her when the silky lining settled intimately over her shoulders. The silk was warm from Logan's body heat and the very thought that *his* hunky torso had been inside this garment robbed her breath and made her head spin.

Running footsteps erupted on the pavement behind them and Logan, immediately alert, kept his arm protectively around her. But their pursuers turned out to be a group of young people, running and laughing to catch the last ferry. Logan's arm remained there and Sally thought there was every chance her knees might give way before they reached the car.

'Keep the jacket on,' he said as he opened the car door for her.

She looked up and her breathing faltered when she saw his face in the faint moonlight.

This isn't a date. He's out of my league.

Nevertheless, the emotion shimmering in Logan's eyes stole Sally's breath. A shadow fell as he dipped his head closer and she knew that he was going to kiss her.

Her senses reached out to him. Instinctively, she lifted her lips just a fraction…

'Sally,' he whispered and his dark gaze devoured her, roving from her hair to her eyes, to her mouth, her white throat.

His hand lifted to touch her hair and Sally held her breath. Her blood hummed with anticipation. Every cell in her waited…

But then she saw sadness—unmistakably—in his eyes. With a gruff, thick-throated sound, he dropped his hand and stepped back abruptly.

Mortified, Sally scrambled into the car and pulled the door shut before Logan could attend to it. Fighting silly tears of disappointment, she scolded herself for being so foolish. Of course she understood that Logan couldn't kiss her. How could he when they'd both spent the entire evening making a song and dance about the fact that he was her boss and this was not a date?

When they reached her house, he walked her to the door, but she didn't ask him in.

'Thanks for your jacket,' she said as she handed it to him. 'And thanks for a lovely evening.'

'My pleasure, Sally. Thanks for your company.' About to return to his car, he said, 'I should have checked my diary. I'll let you know on Monday about the next lesson. Is that all right?'

If she was sensible, she would have told him that she couldn't manage any more dancing lessons. She was quite sure she couldn't endure more time alone with him. But he'd just bought her a lavish meal. And, honestly, even though she knew it was pointless to love him, how could she bear to give him up?

'Sure,' she said softly. 'You still need some more polish. Let me know on Monday.'

When he reached her front gate, she called, 'Have a good weekend.'

'Thanks, Sally. You, too.'

As she went inside, she thought, *I'm not sure that's possible.*

Memories of that moment when Logan had *almost* kissed her reverberated in Sally's awareness all weekend. As a distraction, she invited Anna and the children over for Sunday lunch and afterwards they all went to a park by the harbour, played on the swings, fed the ducks and generally had a good time. Sally fought off memories of that time she'd seen her boss playing in the park with his nephews.

On Monday morning, Logan arrived at Blackcorp with his mobile phone welded to his ear. He gave Sally a hurried nod as he sped past her, then disappeared.

So…it was business as usual. *What else did I expect?*

She was a fool to be disappointed.

Maeve bounced in with a smile that spread from ear to ear. She and her geologist had spent a weekend away in the Blue Mountains and it had been *so-o-o* romantic. Sally tried not to feel jealous, with little success.

Maeve was in the middle of describing a marble spa bath set in a bay window overlooking the Megalong Valley when Maria Paige swept through the security door.

Sally couldn't explain why, but something about the boss's PA bothered her. She always felt on edge whenever Maria was around.

Pushing past Maeve, as if she were invisible, Maria dumped a pile of computer disks on the desk in front of Sally. 'Can you be a darling, Sally, and download these on to a file on your computer?'

A darling? Sally choked back an exclamation. What was this about? She knew her job description didn't include working under the direction of Logan's personal assistant. Just the same, she wanted to please this woman. Maria was the only person in the company who sent off negative vibes and Sally certainly didn't want to make an enemy of her.

'Don't look so worried, Sally. I just need a backup. For security.'

'Of course. I'll get on to it straight away.'

With a thin smile, Maria spun around and, ignoring Maeve again, marched back through the security door.

Maeve watched in silence until she'd gone, then gave an expressive roll of her eyes. 'It might be wise to remember that you're a very small finch.'

'What are you talking about?'

'That one's a predator, and a dangerous one at that.'

'Oh, come on, Maeve. That's a bit mean. Maria's a bit sharp, but I suspect she's under a lot of pressure, working for someone like Logan…I…I mean Mr Black.'

Maeve shook her head slowly. 'I've been watching that woman for two years and I'm still waiting for her to pounce. You be careful with her, my girl.'

She tapped her nose knowingly and walked on, but her

warning echoed like a menacing alarm bell as Sally loaded the first disk and started saving Maria's files.

In the middle of the afternoon, however, any niggles of disquiet about Maria's request flew out of her head when the boss telephoned.

'I hope this isn't too late notice, but would tomorrow evening suit you for another dancing lesson?'

Sally knew she should give him an excuse. Could she really go through another night of self-torture? Perhaps she should tell him she was babysitting Oliver and Rose.

But it would be a lie and Sally was terminally honest. Logan needed at least one more lesson. How could she let him down?

Miserably aware that she was inviting another round of heartache, she assured him that Tuesday evening was fine.

This wasn't working.

Halfway through the second dancing lesson, Logan's concentration was shot to pieces.

It was crazy, really, because tonight's session should have been so much easier than the first one. Not only had he one or two clues about waltzing now, but Sally had been considerate enough to abandon the dangerous low-backed yellow dress in favour of a simple T-shirt and boyish jeans.

Her shirt was high-necked with long sleeves, so Logan was spared the distraction of her bare, soft and silky skin. But, even though she was clothed from neck to toe, Sally Finch still provided far too many distractions. Logan's fingers could sense the supple warmth of her through the T-shirt's thin fabric, could smell her clean hair, her fresh, fragrant skin.

This close, she made him too painfully conscious of the lush invitation of her lips, smiling mere inches from his.

But the worst torment came from his own clumsiness,

which caused him to bump, every so often, against her. Each brush against Sally was like a teasing promise, each brief point of contact a burning fiery brand.

If this went on much longer, Logan feared he might self-combust.

In the past, if he'd been aroused by a woman, he would have moved swiftly to seduce her. In the past, he'd always been able to steer his desires towards suitable women who were as pragmatic as he was about balancing their desires with the demands of their careers.

In the past, Logan had not met Sally.

Sweet, warm and dangerous Sally.

He feared, at some deeply primitive level, that if he took Sally to his bed, he would want to keep her there for ever. And that wasn't part of the game plan.

'Logan, lead with your body, not with your feet,' Sally's voice commanded from somewhere below his ear.

Sweat trickled down the back of his neck. If he led with his body, he would bump into her again.

'Look to the left to watch where you're going.'

Logan looked to his left and he twirled her as lightly and deftly as he could.

'Smile!' cried Sally.

'I can't.'

That was asking too much.

To his relief, the music they'd been dancing to came to an end and Sally stopped. 'That was great, wasn't it?'

'Do you think so?' He was sure he'd made next to no progress.

'Oh, yes.' She spoke soothingly—a teacher calming an over-anxious pupil. 'I think you've almost mastered the waltz.'

Crossing to the player plugged into the wall, she said, 'Have you thought about any other dances you'd like to learn?'

'Other dances?'

'You're going to spend an entire evening at the ball and you can't waltz the whole time.'

'But I'm only dancing the one dance for the charity.'

'Oh, Logan, don't be silly. You can't stand out for the whole evening.'

'Can't I?'

'Everyone else will be dancing. Your partner will expect you to dance with her. That's what balls are all about.'

Exactly. And he'd been tardy about finding a partner for this function. Apart from the fact that he thought of it as an ordeal that had to be endured, he'd delayed his invitation because no one on his usual list of female companions had *felt* right. Carissa had rung at the weekend to warn him, somewhat heatedly, that he was running out of time.

Sally fiddled with the player, pressing buttons until she found different music. A bright and modern and up-tempo sound erupted, filling the room with its brassy, foot-tapping beat.

Swaying and nodding in time to it, Sally sent him a cheeky grin. 'What about trying a little of the old disco shuffle? Just to loosen up? You've been to nightclubs, surely?'

'Occasionally, but do they allow that kind of dancing at balls?' He had to raise his voice to reach her above the thumping noise.

'I'd be surprised if they didn't include some. It is the twenty-first century, after all.' Arms above her head, Sally jiggled and shook, making her bright curls bounce. 'Come on, Logan. Let me see what you've got.'

He would have liked to simply stand there and watch Sally. She was so lively and pretty, so graceful and glowing. She shimmied up to him, swaying her lithe body and holding her hands out in front of her. 'Just move. You can stay in one spot if you like, but get those feet going.'

Logan nodded his head and started to move self-consciously.

'Close your eyes,' she instructed. 'Forget I'm here. Just listen to the music and feel that beat.'

It certainly helped to close his eyes. Without the distraction of Sally in front of him, he could hear the pumping rhythm, the throb of the bass, pounding in time to his accelerated heartbeat.

'Now let yourself go,' Sally urged. 'Loosen your shoulders and go with the flow.'

Her voice was surprisingly close and, when he opened his eyes, he found her bobbing and swaying beside him. 'Come on,' she coaxed with another glowing smile, 'forget you're the boss and just hang loose.'

Taking his hands in hers, Sally drew him gently towards her. That did it. The temptation was too much. Forget dancing! Logan closed the gap between them, gathered Sally in and kissed her.

CHAPTER TEN

SALLY stopped dancing. Her entire system stopped, stilled by the sweet shock of Logan's lips touching hers.

A moment's fear claimed her as she remembered that other time, that *other* man she'd danced with and that other kiss that had turned so quickly into a nightmare.

A wave of panic rose instinctively. But then, thankfully, reason kicked in.

This man wasn't remotely like Kyle Francis. This was Logan, the man she'd been fantasising about for weeks now. She knew him well. She'd been alone with him many times. She'd met his grandmother, for heaven's sake, and she really, really wanted his kiss.

Winding her arms about Logan's neck, her hesitation dissolved. There was no more doubt, no fear—just an amazing melting happiness. Logan's lips were tender and sensuous, his kiss unhurried, almost lazy, as if he knew her worst fears and how to allay them with one perfect, sensuous, dizzying kiss.

Twining his hand in her hair, he tilted her head back so that he could take the kiss deeper while his other hand supported the small of her back, holding her against him, which was just as well because her body and her legs were melting faster than sugar in hot tea.

Never had she felt so safe, yet sexy. She wanted to wrap herself around Logan. She wanted to—

His body stiffened suddenly and he lifted his mouth from hers.

Dazed, disappointed, Sally blinked and saw that he was glaring in the direction of the door. The *open* door.

The security guard was standing there, confusion and embarrassment in his eyes. He said something that they couldn't hear above the blare of the music. Sally hurried to turn it off.

The sudden silence was shocking.

'I—I'm terribly sorry, Mr Black.' The guard was red-faced as he scratched at the top of his bald head. 'I heard the music and I thought some kids had broken in.'

Logan didn't reply. He stood there with his hands on his hips, staring with a narrowed, angry gaze in the direction of the door. Clearly, he hated this moment and it was Sally's fault. She'd played the rowdy music. She'd taunted him with her come-and-get-me dancing.

'It's OK, Reg,' Logan said at last. 'There's no problem here. We're just finishing up.'

'I'll be on my way, then.' The guard's eyes were still wide with disbelief as he exited backwards, pulling the door closed as he went.

Logan turned and his gaze met Sally's. Her heart thumped as they stood watching each other without speaking. It was an age before he reacted and then his mouth tilted into a tiny lopsided smile. 'I'm sorry,' he said quietly. 'I shouldn't have kissed you.'

So that was how it was going to be. He would dismiss it as a mistake, easily forgotten. Sally managed to turn her sigh of disappointment into a casual shrug. 'It doesn't matter.' She forced a cheerful smile. 'We can blame it on the music.'

He seemed relieved that she was happy to leave it at that.

'I guess we've done enough for tonight,' he said. 'I should take you home now.'

Her mind was reeling from the double shock of his kiss and its interruption and she simply nodded and unplugged the player from the wall.

They walked back to the car in silence.

Before Logan turned on the ignition, he said, 'If you open the glove box, you'll find a CD that I thought might interest you. I meant to show it to you earlier.'

Sally took it out and read the label. '*Hattie Lane at the Piano*. Is this your grandmother's music?'

He nodded and set the car in motion, reversing smoothly out of the parking space.

'I'd love to hear Hattie play. Can we listen to this now?'

'You're welcome to borrow it.'

The car shot out into the busy lanes of traffic and Sally stared at Logan's handsome profile. What an enigma he was—one minute distancing himself from her and behaving as if their kiss was nothing more than a careless mistake, and then suddenly opening a door into his private life and offering to share something of deep personal significance. Did he realise he was sending her so many mixed signals?

When he pulled up outside her house, he said, 'About the ball.'

Sally hoped he wasn't going to ask for another lesson. How could she stand the stress of pretending this was just about business? She'd already breached her personal pain threshold.

But the question of lessons wasn't raised. Instead, Logan looked at her and continued calmly, as if he were discussing the weather, 'I thought you might like to come to the ball. As my partner.'

This time Sally didn't just stare, she gasped. Several times. Logan had, quite literally, taken her breath away.

'You've told me how much you love balls and this is a truly

glittering event,' he added with a smile that was pure Prince Charming. 'And I can't think of anyone I know who'd enjoy this ball as much as you would.'

'But…I…we…'

'Don't you think you've earned it, Sally?'

Her mouth opened and shut. She was quite sure she should refuse him loudly and promptly, and her inability to do this immediately was frightening. Her best defence against this boss, who sent her so many confusing signals, was to stay well clear.

His right hand tightened around the steering wheel. 'To be honest, I should confess that the whole Diana Devenish thing still terrifies me and I could do with a little moral support.' He shot her another of his gorgeous smiles. 'A comrade in arms, so to speak.'

Sally gulped. 'Like a coach, cheering you on from the sidelines?'

'Exactly.'

Oh, help. She feared she was weakening. 'But—but a ball's very public. If I went as your partner, everyone at Blackcorp would be bound to find out.'

'I'd say that cat's already out of the bag. The security fellow is bound to talk.' He shrugged and his jaw squared as he stared out through the windscreen at a rubbish bin that someone had forgotten to take back inside. 'So what do you think?'

'I…I don't know.' Her mind seemed to have frozen. But one sure thing she couldn't ignore was that Logan Black needed her help.

Looking down, she saw Hattie's CD in her hands. There was a picture on the cover of an elegant dark-eyed woman seated at the piano in a slinky silver gown. She was aged about forty and barely recognisable as Logan's elderly grandmother. Sally stared at the glamorous photograph and, thinking aloud, said, 'I don't have anything to wear.'

He chuckled. 'That's easily fixed. There's a woman in Rose Bay with a fabulous dress shop. If I send you to Agathe, she'll kit you out.'

Rose Bay? The prices in those shops were exorbitant.

'And I'll take care of the bill,' he said.

'But you can't. I couldn't let you.'

'Don't waste your breath fighting that one, Sally. It's payment where payment is due. If you help me to get through this ghastly ball, you'll be doing me an enormous favour.'

'It would be much easier to say yes if you hadn't kissed me tonight.'

Jerking his gaze away down the street again, Logan said, 'That's a fair comment, but as a boss speaking to an employee, I give you my word, Sally.' His hand on the steering wheel clenched tighter. 'I'm not a louse and I will not expect you to sleep with me as payment for a ticket to the ball.'

Sally's cheeks grew very hot. 'Right. I…I didn't expect that you would.' She swallowed to relieve the sudden dryness in her throat. 'But it…it's helpful to be clear about it.' She realised she was trembling, but not with fear. She could trust this man; she knew that.

The long conversations at the team-building workshop, the hours they'd spent dancing, the visit to Hattie's, the dinner, the kiss—never once had Logan shown any reason why she should be afraid of him.

His gaze flicked over her and she saw a small gleam of amusement in his eyes.

'What's so funny?'

'I can't believe I'm putting such a lovely girl off limits.'

Off limits? Sally was startled by her disappointment. She might not fear this man, but perhaps being in love with him was a worse problem. She longed to tell him that being 'off limits' wasn't what she wanted at all. In fact, his gentlemanly declaration made her utterly miserable. The more she saw of Logan, the more deeply she fell for him. She should never have let her feelings get this far.

'Is that settled, then?' he asked her, annoyingly calm. 'Will you come with me to the ball?'

Sally could feel her resistance giving way. Romantic yearnings aside, she felt a teacherly pride in her pupil. Logan had tried really hard to learn how to waltz and he'd made terrific progress. She would love watching him pull off the dance with Diana Devenish.

'Take pity on me, Sally.'

'The last thing you need, Mr Black, is pity.'

'Think of your own enjoyment, then. You'll love it.'

She could almost feel Chloe urging her. *You came to Sydney for opportunities like this.*

'All right,' she said finally, 'I'll come.' With her hand on the door handle, she remembered to add her thanks. And then she remembered something else. 'The ball's on Friday evening, you'll have to make arrangements for Hattie's roses.

Logan smiled warmly. 'Thanks for the reminder. You'd make a great PA.'

In the kitchen, Sally made herself a cup of tea. She added sugar and milk and took it into the lounge room, where she slipped Hattie's CD into the player.

Almost immediately, the gorgeous sounds of a piano rippled and soared and rolled around her. The music was beautiful…like moonlight on water, or the first flush of dawn in the bush. It reached inside Sally, touching soul-deep chords.

'Oh, Hattie,' she whispered, sinking into an armchair, 'I had no idea.'

She pictured Hattie, young and talented and beautiful, and she saw Logan as a little boy playing in his grandmother's garden where white roses bloomed. Deep inside, she felt a bond with them. She thought of Hattie now, old and frail; Logan tall and manly.

Ridiculously, for no reason that she properly understood, she began to cry.

The next evening she telephoned Clifton House and asked if she could speak to Hattie Lane.

'Hello,' answered a quavering voice.

'Hattie?'

'Yes.'

'It's Sally Finch. Logan lent me one of your CDs and I wanted to tell you how much I loved it.'

'Thank you, Sally. How thoughtful of you to call.'

'I think your playing is absolutely brilliant. So beautiful. It made me cry. In the nicest possible way.'

'Well, thank you, dear.' After a beat, Hattie asked, 'Did you say that Logan gave you the CD?'

'Yes.'

'My, my.' Hattie sounded amused. 'And I believe you're going to the Hospital Ball with him.'

Gosh. Word got around quickly. 'Yes, I am. Did Logan tell you about it?'

'His sister, Carissa, rang me earlier this afternoon. When I told her that I'd already met you here at Clifton House, she was agog.' Hattie laughed. 'You've really set the cat among the pigeons, Sally.'

'Actually, that would be a Finch, not a cat.'

Hattie laughed harder, but then she said, much more soberly, 'You will be careful, won't you, my dear?'

'I…I'm not sure what you mean.'

'I see. Then perhaps I'd better leave well alone.'

'No, please don't. If there's something I should know, I'd like you to tell me.'

After a disconcerting silence, Hattie said, 'My grandson would never hurt you intentionally, Sally. He's a dear boy and incredibly generous. If it weren't for his assistance, I wouldn't be able to stay in this expensive nursing home and his parents wouldn't be tripping around Australia. But I'm afraid he's far too focused on his business. He's intent on making sure he doesn't commit the same mistakes his father made.'

Sally would have liked to ask what those mistakes were, but that would have been too nosy.

'It would take someone quite exceptional to steer Logan away from the course he's set upon,' Hattie said. 'But then, I suspect that you are an exceptional girl, Sally.'

If Sally had been better acquainted with Hattie, if she'd been having this conversation face to face rather than over the telephone, she might have pressed the elderly woman for an explanation. What was this course that Logan had embarked on and why should anyone want to steer him from it?

As she hung up, she wondered if Logan's grandmother assumed that all girls who went out with her grandson heard wedding bells.

'Not this girl,' Sally said, replacing the receiver thoughtfully. 'I might be fanciful but I have both feet firmly on the ground.'

CHAPTER ELEVEN

IT WAS six o'clock and Logan was still working at his desk. Each time he looked up, the waters of Sydney Harbour were a little darker. Now the street lights had come on and headlights glowed in the purpling twilight. Traffic on the bridge looked like bright strings of beads, as cars headed for home.

He should be heading off too, but he wanted to finish this proposal first. He preferred to stay back and get work finished, keeping his home as his refuge, his haven from the battlefield of business.

Another fifteen minutes should do it. Logan turned back to the list of figures on his computer screen.

'Knock, knock!'

The unexpected voice at his office door startled him. 'Sally!' His smile was spontaneous. These days, he only had to *think* about Sally and he started smiling. 'What are you doing here at this late hour?'

'I was waiting to speak to you.'

'Really?' His throat constricted and he had to swallow. 'I—I'm sorry if I've kept you waiting. I had some work to clear up.' He frowned at her. 'But you didn't have to stay back. Maria knows I have an open door policy with my staff. Or you could have telephoned.'

Sally dropped her gaze to something she was holding and he saw that it was a CD. 'I needed to be certain that no one will overhear our conversation,' she said.

'I see.' A disquieting thought struck. 'You're still coming to the ball, aren't you?'

'Yes.' She looked up and her gaze softened. 'I wouldn't pull out at this late stage.' She looked suddenly animated. 'I've got my dress. It's gorgeous.'

'I'm glad you like it.'

She waved the CD. 'I'm afraid this is a business matter.'

'You'd better take a seat, then.' He wished it wasn't so hard to be formal and businesslike with Sally. He kept thinking about kissing her.

'Is it OK if I shut the door?'

'If you insist.' Logan's frown deepened. What on earth was this about?

Sally pulled out a chair and sat. She was wearing a bright blue top and a neat grey skirt. Ordinary, everyday working clothes which shouldn't have looked incredibly sexy. On her they did. Intensely so, especially when she crossed her legs with an unconscious grace that robbed him of oxygen.

For days he'd been trying to forget how she'd felt in his arms—soft and sensuous and willing. She'd completely wrecked his powers of concentration.

'So what did you want to discuss?' His voice was gruffer than he'd intended.

'This.' Sally set the CD on the desk. But she didn't speak immediately. She looked worried, almost embarrassed, and chewed at her lower lip. Her soft, pink, infinitely kissable lower lip. 'Can you confirm that it's OK for me to send off the contents of this disk to an outside email? Maria said it was an urgent job for you, but she had a problem with her own computer and I wanted to—'

'Maria?' Logan interrupted. 'Did you say Maria asked you to send emails?'

'Yes.'

'Why?'

'She said she was having trouble with the Internet. She's been getting me to do odd jobs. The other day she asked me to save a whole stack of files on to my computer.'

'She *what*?'

Sally squirmed uncomfortably in her chair. 'I feel terrible speaking about your PA behind her back. It's probably fine. She said it was for security. An extra backup.'

No, it wasn't fine. Logan felt stirrings of alarm. 'We have good backup procedures. Maria didn't need to use your computer.'

Sally shrugged unhappily. 'I knew there was no real harm in saving a few files.' She shook her head. 'But I didn't feel right about sending an email when I hadn't been told anything about it.'

Uneasily, Logan asked, 'So what's on the CD?'

'I don't know and I didn't think it was my business to read the files. That's why I wanted to check with you. It seemed odd, like agreeing to take a parcel on an international flight without knowing the contents.'

'Let's have a look, then.' Grim-faced, he picked up the CD and slid it into his computer.

A click of the mouse later, the list of files scrolled on to his screen and the bottom dropped from his stomach.

Sally leaned anxiously across the desk. She'd seen the shock in Logan's eyes and the colour drain from his face and now she felt sick. 'What is it?'

'This is full of information that's come straight from the boardroom. It's supposed to be locked away on a secure file.'

Logan loosened his tie as if he needed more air and Sally saw, with dismay, that his hand was shaking.

He clicked on another file and a groan escaped him. 'This is Blackcorp's strategy for the next three years. It…it's the heart and soul of my company.'

'But—' Sally struggled to take this in. It was so much worse than she'd feared. It sounded disastrous.

Logan lifted his hands to his head and shuddered. 'You haven't sent any of this information, have you?'

'No. Nothing.' She was so glad she could reassure him.

'Good girl.' He let out a heavy sigh. 'In the wrong hands, this would allow a competitor to second guess the next critical stage in Blackcorp's development.' Beckoning to her, he said, 'Look, come and see for yourself. It lists all our company contacts. Key strategies. Pricing.'

She came around to his side of the desk, saw the lists of figures, saw the haggard fear in Logan's eyes.

Thank heavens she'd followed her instincts and double-checked with him.

'Where were you supposed to send this?' he asked.

'I have the list of addresses here.' She pulled the sheet of paper with Maria's list from her pocket.

Logan took one glance at it and let out a groan, then leapt to his feet and released a strong expletive. 'I can't believe Maria did this.'

He could feel panic rising and he began to pace.

'She would have reduced me to my bottom dollar.' He reached the far wall, paced back again. Fear. The sickening fear that had dogged him since his teens clawed at his throat.

He slammed a fist into the wall. 'She must have been a plant all along. She's probably been planning this for ages.

There could have been a takeover of Blackcorp.' It was his worst nightmare.

He shot Sally a fierce glance, challenging her, needing her to understand. 'My family's already been through one bankruptcy. I swore I would never let it happen again in my lifetime.'

All his years of hard work, all his self-denial and disciplined planning would have come to nothing. *Nothing!*

'But everything's OK, isn't it?' Sally asked quietly. 'I didn't send the emails. Nobody got this information.'

'You're right.' Logan shot her a shaky smile. 'You've pulled us back from the brink of disaster.' He felt a blast of euphoria. Sweet, piercing relief. But it quickly evaporated as the full implications of Maria's treachery struck home.

'Maria was setting you up, Sally.' It was a terrible possibility, but it had to be true. 'She wanted the emails to come from you. Then, if the leaks were discovered, they would have been traced to your desk.'

Sally pouted. 'Why did she pick on me?'

'She would have been confident that you didn't have a hope of defending yourself. It's so much easier to cast suspicion on the newest employee.'

'And then it would have been my word against the word of the boss's trusted PA.'

'Exactly.'

This time it was Sally who swore. Colourfully. And then she quickly blushed. 'Sorry. Having four brothers expands a girl's vocabulary. But how dare she use me like that?'

Tears shone in her eyes and the sight of them undid Logan. Closing the gap between them, he took her hands. 'Maria's a poor judge of character. No doubt she thought of you as nothing more than the new girl—a little nobody on the front desk—too terrified to question her.'

Sally rolled her eyes and the action sent her tears spilling down her cheeks. Logan wiped them gently with his thumbs. He said softly, 'Sally saves the day.' It was supposed to make her smile. Her smiles were precious. Pure gold. 'I mean it, Sally. You've saved my company, you've saved me.'

She rewarded him with a tiny tilt of her mouth. Her lovely, soft, inviting mouth. Which he should not be looking at with shameless desire.

But desire for Sally had become his constant companion lately and now it was heightened by all the other emotions swirling through him—shock, horror, gratitude, elation. 'How can I ever thank you?' he whispered and then, to cover the deeper feelings he hadn't meant to reveal, he tried to lighten the moment. 'I'm great with flowers and dinners, but what else can I offer you, Sally?'

For ages she stood there, staring at his computer, but when she looked up there was a playful twinkle in her eyes. 'I think the least you could do is kiss me again.'

Wrong answer. He was supposed to be keeping his distance from this woman. He was her boss and he'd as good as promised that he wouldn't lay a finger on her.

Sally seemed to have forgotten. And, the truth was, Sally had earned twenty years' worth of kisses, and it was only fitting that he should be the man who gave them to her. Slowly. Lovingly. Over every inch of her soft, silky skin.

Whoa, there. Straighten your thinking, man.

Logan shifted his focus from Sally's tempting mouth to the bank of windows. The world outside was pitch-black now. It was time to get her home before he forgot his good intentions. Time to…

He looked into Sally's eyes again. *Major mistake.* He felt as if he were drowning, feared he was losing the fight. He was a mere male and how could he resist this tempting saviour? Why should he resist her when she was so clearly inviting him to kiss her?

Lifting his hands, Logan framed her face, knew he had no chance in this lifetime of keeping his distance.

Nevertheless…it was supposed to be a restrained kiss. That was the plan. Cradling her face with gentle hands, he lowered his lips slowly, brushed them softly against her mouth.

And his plan turned to dust as Sally gave a small whimpering cry, wound her arms around his neck and arched into him. Her lips were sweet and eager. She nipped him lightly on his lower lip and made soft sounds of wanting that sent his best intentions scattering into the night.

His kiss turned hard and deep. His hands slid down her arms and cupped her bottom. *Oh, God.* Her kisses were way beyond sexy. She tasted divine, sent him wild.

He'd never been stirred to this feverish point where physical need and tender emotions were fused in one overwhelming torrent of longing. He had to have this woman. He was on the edge of losing control completely.

No. Hell, no. He couldn't do that.

Somehow Logan found the strength to break the kiss. Sally's cheeks were flushed and her eyes were dark and roused. Touching a finger to her lips, he whispered, 'We shouldn't be doing this. I gave you my word.'

Her chin lifted and her eyes were a clear blue challenge. 'Please don't send me away, Logan.'

'Oh, Sally.' He drew her against him, pressing a kiss into her glorious, sun-bright curls. 'What am I going to do with you?'

'I thought you were doing just fine.'

He groaned softly, knew that he'd lost this particular battle. 'Not here.'

'Where are we going?' Sally asked as the car purred through the forest of skyscrapers in Sydney's city centre.

'My place.'

Logan's quiet answer sent a jolt through her that almost launched her out of her seat.

'Is that OK?' he asked, shooting her an anxious sideways glance.

'Yes. Absolutely.' Her voice was surprisingly calm and confident considering that Logan Black was taking her home, almost certainly to make love to her. She closed her eyes as the impact of this washed over her, bringing wave after wave of shivery excitement.

It was so hard to believe this was actually happening. But it felt right—perfectly right. The whole 'boss' façade had fallen away this evening and Sally had seen a man facing his greatest fear.

Even if she hadn't already been totally smitten by his good looks, or touched by the way he'd tried so earnestly to learn to dance, and with the way he bought white roses for his grandmother, and a thousand other sweet things about him, she would have fallen head over heels tonight.

Tonight, she'd looked into his eyes and she'd seen his soul stripped bare. His vulnerability had given her new courage. She longed to offer him comfort, support, strength, humour—whatever he needed. Everything she had. Heart and body and soul.

He turned off the street and drove into the ground floor garage of a tall apartment block, a pillar of glass and steel. A flurry of nervous excitement rose from Sally's stomach to her throat. Logan turned to her and smiled gorgeously, and she took a deep breath.

'Let me guess,' she said. 'You live on the top floor.'

'I do. I hope you're not afraid of heights.'

'I'm absolutely terrified of them.'

About to get out of the car, he hesitated and looked concerned.

Sally grinned. 'Only joking.'

'Minx. I'll bet you climbed all the tallest gum trees when you were a kid.' Reaching out, he pretended to cuff her cheek, then he leapt out of the car and Sally quickly opened her door.

As they walked to the lift, Logan took her hand and she could feel the warmth of him running through her like a current.

He gave her hand a gentle squeeze and smiled. 'You OK?'

Her only reply was to squeeze *his* hand.

They were alone in the lift as it climbed upwards and he drew her to him and kissed her cheek. Floating on a cloud of desire, she turned in his arms, lifted her lips for another kiss and Logan obliged with enchanting slowness.

'Now that we're being honest with each other, I can tell you that's been a recent fantasy of mine,' she murmured against his jaw.

'To be kissed in the lift?'

'To be kissed by my *boss* in the lift.'

He chuckled. The lift doors slid open and they stepped out. Sally's heart drummed as Logan swiped a plastic tag over a keypad and the door to his penthouse opened.

It was like stepping into a movie set. Logan's open-plan penthouse was stunning, with acres of white carpet, über-modern furniture and sleekly minimalist kitchen fittings. Discreet mood lighting and walls of glass revealed the magic of inner Sydney's nightscape.

Sally looked about her with wide-eyed delight. 'Wow! This is fabulous.' His home was the complete opposite of Chloe's cosy town house and yet, despite its grandeur, Sally thought it offered a sense of welcome and surprising serenity.

'This place suits my needs for the moment.' Logan reached for her hands. 'Are you hungry? My housekeeper leaves frozen meals. I could zap something in the microwave. Do you like Vietnamese food?'

'I don't know,' Sally said. 'I've never tried it, but I'm sure it's delicious.' She looked at him from beneath lowered lashes. 'But I'm not really hungry.' *Not for food.*

He took the hint and drew her closer. 'So, tell me, have you ever been kissed in a penthouse?'

'Never,' she whispered, slipping into his arms easily, happily.

He nuzzled her ear and sent delicious shivers scampering over her skin. 'Is it one of your fantasies?'

'I've just added it to my list.'

Her eyes drifted closed as he kissed her with lazy and tantalising thoroughness.

'Nice,' she murmured dreamily. 'Now, what's *your* fantasy?'

He chuckled. 'You're taking a risk, aren't you?'

'I don't think so, Logan. I trust you.' How wonderful it was to be able to say that.

For a moment the amusement in his eyes faded. Gently, he traced the curve of her cheek. 'I hope I deserve your trust, Sally.'

She gave him a playful punch in the midriff. 'Stop worrying.'

'I can't help feeling responsible for you.'

'I'm a grown woman. You're supposed to feel *lust* for me.'

'That's a guaranteed certainty.' He tucked a curl behind her ear. 'I'll happily share my fantasy with you. It'll only take a minute to organise.'

Scant minutes later, Sally was curled beside him on a big red sofa with a glass of chilled wine in her hand, while the rich and glorious sounds of the Brahms violin concerto rolled over them.

'I've listened to this music every night since we talked about it at the team-building workshop,' he told her. 'And I imagined you here, listening to it too.'

Stunned, she set her shaking glass down on the coffee table. Every night? It was incredible that Logan had been thinking about her all this time. Incredibly fabulous.

'And…and what did I do?' she asked. 'In your fantasy?'

'Oh, you sat very close.' With his arm around her shoulders, he kissed the top of her head. The gorgeous music swelled and soared above and around them and Sally closed her eyes and nestled against him. He smelled so good—a musky male scent mixed with the clean fragrance of his laundered shirt.

The music slowed to the especially beautiful section they both loved. They sat listening and to Sally the notes were like kisses caressing her skin…here…and here…and here…

And here…

'I think Brahms must have been in love when he wrote this music,' she said.

'It's very possible. He fell in love quite regularly.'

'Did he ever marry?'

'No. Apparently, he had a terminal problem with commitment.'

'Oh.' Sally shrugged that aside. Men with commitment phobias were not something she wanted to think about right now.

Logan's fingers sifted through her curls. 'Your hair is such an amazing colour and it's so silky and soft.' His deep voice had turned husky.

'I'm rather keen on your chin.' She pressed a kiss against his stubbled jaw. 'It's so raspy and rough.'

The music wound higher and higher, mimicking the tightening coil of desire inside her. 'Logan, I do hope you made love to me in this fantasy.'

'Oh, Sally!'

He pulled her closer, sealed her mouth with his and desire flamed between them with the speed of fire in dry grass. Suddenly they were kissing and touching with reckless fervour. Sally arched into Logan and his hands slipped under her blouse. His thumbs brushed the tight peaks of her breasts and longing pooled inside her.

Her cry of need echoed his and, in the next heartbeat, they were frantically helping each other out of their clothes.

Sally and Logan lay naked, their bodies loose and relaxed in the aftermath of their lovemaking.

'Thank you,' she murmured as she nestled her head on Logan's shoulder and watched the moon reach through the high circular window to cast interesting patterns over their bodies. 'You've no idea how grateful I am.'

He chuckled softly and his hand settled on her waist. With a slow possessive action, he traced the pale, moonlit curve from her waist to her hip. 'I'm sure the gratitude is mutual, Sally.'

'I'm not just talking about sex.' Sally took a quick breath. It was time to tell this man who'd just made sweetly tender and passionate love to her that he'd released her fear. 'I had a bad experience at a dance. I was almost raped and—'

Logan's hand stilled.

'—I've been frightened of men,' Sally told him.

He sat up swiftly. 'That's terrible. Why didn't you tell me?'

'I—I didn't want to scare you off.'

'You poor girl. If I'd known about that I would have been more gentle with you.'

'You were gentle, Logan. You were perfect.' She took his hands. 'I must confess something.'

'Something else? What is it?' His voice sounded choked, as if he'd swallowed pebbles.

'Coming to Sydney has been a bit of an experiment.'

'I've been part of an experiment?'

'Sort of. But I didn't plan it that way. I came here to prove to my family that I'm OK now. They were getting too worried about me—tiptoeing around me, treating me like a patient. When Chloe left me her house, I'm afraid I rather jumped at the chance to escape. And then, when you asked me to help you with the dancing lessons, I realised you'd offered me the perfect chance to face up to my fears.'

Logan's face was in shadow so she couldn't see his reaction, but then he leaned forward into the puddle of moonlight and his grim and strained expression betrayed his shock. 'You took a terrible risk, Sally.'

'Not really.'

'I might have been as bad as the mongrel who attacked you.'

'You sound like my brothers.' Lifting his hands to her lips, she kissed them. 'Right from the day you fell in the duck pond, I knew you were really nice.'

'Nice? I hate that word.'

She shrugged. 'Now you're pretending to be tough again, when you're really a softie.' With her fingertip, she traced his jaw line and it was anything but soft. 'Seriously, Logan, you really have helped me more than you could guess. Getting to know you, learning to trust you, having you make love to me—it's all been—'

'Therapeutic?' Logan supplied as she searched for the right word.

Sally laughed, then dropped her head to press kisses into the shadowy base of his neck. 'Honestly, Logan, you're better than any therapy.' She let her voice sound sultry.

Releasing a soft sound, half growl, half sigh, he gathered her in and whispered in her ear, 'Honestly, Sally, I'd recommend a little more of my therapy.'

She smiled in the darkness, snuggled closer. 'Isn't honesty the best thing?'

Logan woke early to the sounds of morning traffic rising from the streets below and to an unfamiliar sense of well-being.

Beside him, Sally slept soundly. She looked impossibly young and defenceless as she lay there, with her bright curls tumbling over the pillow and the white sheet pushed aside to reveal one sweet, pink-tipped breast. He thought again about what she'd told him about the mongrel at the dance and he was gripped by an overwhelming desire to protect her.

But that urge was tempered by an equally irresistible desire to wake Sally. A few soft kisses would stir her and she would roll towards him, welcoming the new day with more love-making—open, honest, tender-sweet, unabashed lovemaking.

Logan sighed heavily. That exquisite pleasure would have to be set aside for now. It was Friday morning and a particularly unpleasant business day awaited him.

He was used to waking every working morning to a sense of pressure and worry, but today he faced particularly unpleasant duties. Maria's quiet but immediate departure had to be arranged, and he had to notify his competitors that he knew what they'd been up to. And he needed to take another careful look at his long-term strategies.

He went through to the kitchen, turned on his coffee machine, then went to the bathroom and shaved and showered.

Sally woke when he came back into the bedroom with a towel around his hips.

She grinned at him, hitched on to one elbow and let her eyes rake over his body with frank admiration and the temptation to dive back into bed with her was almost too much.

Sensing his hesitation, she looked momentarily disappointed, then sniffed the air. 'You've already made coffee. Have I slept in? What time is it?'

'After seven.'

With a groan she rolled to the edge of the bed. 'Will we have time to go via my place so I can get clean clothes before work?'

'If you get a wriggle on.'

'And I'll need breakfast. I can't function on a cup of coffee the way you can, Logan.' In the bathroom doorway, she turned back to him. 'I just remembered we're going to the ball tonight.'

Her teeth flashed white and she sent him an excited smile before she disappeared, but Logan didn't feel nearly so happy. The last thing he needed at the end of this difficult day was the ordeal of dancing in public with Diana Devenish.

CHAPTER TWELVE

SALLY sat in front of her dressing table mirror, wrapped in an old Japanese kimono that had once been Chloe's, and gave her lips a final dab of colour.

After the magic of last night and the strange tension of carrying on at work today as if nothing out of the ordinary had happened, it was almost too exciting to have this evening's ball to look forward to as well.

It had been so hard to behave normally at work. She was so over-the-top in love with Logan she thought she might burst with happiness and she'd half-expected people to take one look at her and know everything about last night.

Mid-morning, Maria Paige had marched past, wearing dark glasses and carrying her briefcase. She'd completely ignored Sally, but her exit had caused a distinctly uncomfortable moment. Luckily, neither Kim nor Maeve knew about Maria's departure, so the subject hadn't come up at lunch time and this evening Sally wanted to think about nothing except the exciting night ahead of her.

She had taken enormous care with her make-up and with the added glamour of upswept curls, courtesy of Patrick the hairdresser from around the corner, she looked like someone in a fashion magazine rather than Sally Finch from Tarra-Binya.

Time to get dressed. The gold lamé dress, selected by Agathe from the shop in Rose Bay, was hanging on the outside of the mahogany wardrobe, shimmering palely as if it were woven from starlight.

Very carefully, Sally lifted it from its hanger and stepped into it, then inched it gently, gently upwards. Butterflies flapped madly in her stomach as the expensive fabric glided silkily up, over her hips and her breasts. She slipped the shoe-string straps over her shoulders, then held her breath as she reached behind and slid the zipper into place.

Cautiously, she executed a little twirl in the middle of the bedroom. Perfect. The gown hugged her like a second skin. But it was oh, so easy to move in. Sally caught sight of her reflection in the mirror and felt a little shiver. Was that glamorous, sexy woman really her?

She was confident that Logan would love this dress, but of course his main focus tonight would be getting through the waltz with Diana Devenish.

OK…now jewellery. She had decided to wear a locket that had been Chloe's—gorgeous antique gold with a pale blue topaz surrounded by tiny pearls.

Lifting the locket from a velvet-lined box, she held it for a sentimental moment, testing the weight of it in her palm. She curled her fingers around it, felt the cool, neat facets of the topaz, the smooth little bumps of the pearls.

If you could see me tonight, Chloe, I think you'd approve.

The heavy locket sat perfectly in the deep V of her neckline and Sally secured matching blue topaz earrings, the exact blue of her eyes. She took a step back and wondered what her parents and brothers would think if they could see their youngest family member now.

They'd be worried, of course, but tonight she knew she was

in safe hands. How wonderful it was to be totally, totally certain that Logan would never do anything to hurt her.

The front doorbell rang.

That will be him.

Stomach aflutter, Sally sent another hasty glance towards the mirror. Hair, make-up, dress. All were as they should be. The blue topaz earrings winked, catching the light. The locket gleamed softly at the base of her throat. The golden dress shimmered.

OK. Nothing more to do here. Scooping up her small clutch bag, she hurried downstairs.

She was prepared for the impact of Logan's total gorgeousness as she opened her front door. At least she thought she was prepared. But she hadn't considered the formal dinner suit factor.

At first, as the door swung open, he was standing with his back to her, looking out into the street. When he turned, she was hit by the cumulative effect of his handsome face and the white shirt front, the neat black bow-tie and the perfectly cut suit.

'Oh! Wow!' she whispered.

'Wow to you, too,' he whispered back. 'Sally, you look amazing.' He stood there with a little bewildered smile lighting his face as his eyes devoured her from head to toe. 'You'll certainly be turning heads tonight.'

'Thanks so much for this dress. I feel as if Agathe has released my inner princess.'

Logan grinned. 'I want to kiss you, but I'd hate to mess you up.' He offered her his elbow. 'Let's go and get this over with.'

He was sick with tension, Sally thought, as she slipped her arm though his and pulled the door shut behind her.

It had rained during the afternoon, leaving the streets slick and shiny so that car tyres swished, sending up fine sprays of water. Cocooned luxuriously within Logan's car, she smiled at him. 'I can understand if you feel a bit nervous.'

'I'm certainly not going to admit to nerves.'

Of course he wouldn't. That was how he would get through tonight. He was a man who'd made an art form of hiding his emotions behind a façade of confidence and strength. It was why he was so successful in business. But she knew there was another side to this man. Deep down he was uneasy, would be relieved when this night was over.

'You're going to be fine,' she told him. 'I can't believe how much progress you've made. You're by far my best pupil.'

'How many pupils have you had?'

'In Sydney? One.'

They both laughed.

'Seriously, Logan, when you take into consideration that you had to force yourself to do something you've never liked, you've achieved a miracle.' They stopped at a set of lights. 'You're going to pull this off because you have a musical ear and you're fiercely competitive.'

She saw the white flash of his grin. 'And I had a fabulous teacher.'

'You've done your share of good turns,' Sally countered, remembering last night and how completely safe and blissfully happy she'd felt in his arms.

They continued on through the rain-washed streets, heading for Woolloomooloo, and then they turned a corner and she saw ahead of them a grand building ablaze with lights. Cars and limousines were lined up in the semicircular driveway in front of the entrance and a crowd had gathered to watch.

Leaning forward, she peered through the windscreen. 'Is that where we're going?'

'Yes, that's the Jameson.'

'Heavens, there are cameramen everywhere. And, oh, my gosh, red carpet!' She whirled sideways. 'I can't believe there's red carpet. It…it's like the Oscars.'

'It's no big deal, Sally. Red carpets are a dime a dozen these days. They use them all the time.'

Porters rushed forward to open their doors and there was even a valet to park the car for them. As Sally emerged into the cool evening, she could hear the faint strains of a dance band coming from inside the hotel. The lights of cameras flashed in her eyes and strangers on the footpath stared.

Logan, close behind her, placed a comforting hand at the small of her back. 'All you have to do is smile and walk.'

Once they were inside, it was clear that this ball was a truly glittering affair. The Jameson Hotel's décor was sumptuous. Huge mirrors hung on the walls, reflecting distinguished men in dashing dinner suits and glamorous women in jewel-bright gowns of every conceivable colour and cut. Dazzling chandeliers hung from high ceilings and a wide, circular expanse of polished flooring shone, awaiting hundreds of dancing feet.

Round tables covered in floor-length white damask had been decorated with arrangements of yellow rosebuds and, above the flowers, white balloons filled with helium were anchored by silver ribbons. The tall fronds of potted palms were glossy and exotic against white marble columns. Rows of wineglasses, soon to be filled, shone like brittle soap bubbles.

For Sally, it was hard not to stare. There were so many 'beautiful people' here, so many famous faces—politicians, TV celebrities and sporting stars and high profile men and women in business. Many of them greeted Logan with back slaps, handshakes, kisses or cries of 'Darling!'

They all seemed delighted to meet Sally, although one or two of the women scrutinised her with surreptitious, sharp-eyed glances.

All around them, the party atmosphere gained momentum. Corks popped and champagne began to flow in frothy gushes. Bottles of red and white wine were opened and glasses filled.

Silver trays appeared, laden with canapés so dainty and colourful they were miniature works of art.

When a strikingly attractive dark-haired woman in a strapless emerald-green gown rushed, arms extended, to greet Logan, Sally wasn't surprised to learn that she was his sister. Carissa's husband, Geoff, a tall man with balding ginger hair and a nice smile, was also introduced.

'I've been dying to meet you, Sally,' Carissa said. 'You're just what the doctor ordered.' Before Sally had time to decipher this comment, Carissa went on, 'And I must congratulate you. Teaching my brother to dance is a magnificent feat. On a par with putting a man on Mars.'

Logan coughed nervously. 'It might be wise to hold back on the congratulations until you're sure I've earned them.'

Watching Logan, Sally caught the quick flash of fear in his eyes. He turned to look out at the huge, shining expanse of the dance floor and she saw the jerky movement of his throat. Reaching for his hand, she gave it a gentle squeeze.

She was rewarded by his smile, especially for her, and she might have basked in its warmth if everyone around them hadn't started turning towards the ballroom's entrance. The babble of voices rose briefly on a wave of excitement and then fell in hushed awe as a tall raven-haired woman with alabaster skin, revealed in vast quantities by a stunning ruby-red gown, entered the room on the arm of a small and balding bespectacled man.

The Air Force concert band trumpeted a fanfare.

'Ladies and gentlemen,' a deep syrupy voice, vaguely familiar to Sally, announced, 'please welcome the Chairman of the Hospital Board, Mr Rupert Sinclair-Jones, and our special guest of honour, Australia's favourite star of dancing, Ms Diana Devenish!'

Applause broke out as Diana Devenish sailed into the

ballroom with the haughty dignity of Cleopatra arriving in Rome.

Logan glanced at Sally, raised his eyebrows and gave her a nervously lopsided grin.

Leaning close to him, she said, 'You'll be fine, Logan. Anyway, tonight's supposed to be about raising money for very sick children. The dancing's just a gimmick.'

He nodded, but he didn't look entirely convinced. Sally looked again at Diana Devenish and noted her perfect deportment and her dancer's body—willow-slender, with a swanlike neck and long limbs. A chill skittered down her spine and she felt swamped by an overwhelming sense of responsibility for Logan's performance. Suddenly, *she* was the one who was churned up and scared.

Was I too casual about this? Should I have asked more questions? She hoped—fervently—that she hadn't let Logan down.

Until this evening, she hadn't really appreciated the huge scale of this ball. She wished she'd insisted that Logan had a dozen lessons from a fully qualified professional ballroom teacher.

But it was too late now. Too late for more lessons and too late for regrets.

The syrupy-voiced MC—a popular radio announcer, Carissa informed Sally—welcomed everyone and introduced the Lord Mayor, who made a more formal speech of welcome. He reminded everyone about the charity raffle, told them how much money had been raised and read out the names of the highest donors.

This was greeted by enthusiastic applause and, when the MC repeated the names of the top three benefactors and announced that they would be dancing with Diana Devenish this evening, the applause became thunderous and accompanied by cheers and whistles.

'See,' Sally whispered, 'you're already a star.'

But Logan looked pale and distinctly ill. He glanced at his wristwatch and sighed and she knew he would rather be anywhere than here.

The music started up—a contemporary number, but with a waltzing beat—and, almost immediately, couples moved on to the dance floor.

Sally turned to Logan. 'Do you recognise the beat?'

He managed a grin. 'How could I miss the old one-two-three, one-two-three?' To her surprise, he reached for her hand. 'Come for a whirl out there,' he said. 'I need a warm-up while there's a crowd and no one's watching.'

'Good idea,' she whispered and, next minute, she was in Logan's arms again, waltzing.

It should have been fun. They'd done this so many times together, but everything was different tonight. The glittering lights overhead, the big band sound of the music, the superfine wool of Logan's dinner jacket beneath Sally's hand. His aftershave. His tanned throat above his crisp white collar.

Logan. So gorgeous. And Sally so deeply and hopelessly in love with him.

Don't think about that now. Concentrate on the dancing.

He smiled at her. 'Am I gliding?'

'Like an ice-skater,' she said.

Carissa, twirling past with Geoff, beamed at them over her husband's shoulder and sent them the thumbs-up sign.

The dance bracket finished. One hurdle over. Logan thanked Sally sincerely, escorted her off the floor and found her a drink. She'd taken two sips before one of Logan's friends asked her to dance.

And that became the pattern of the next hour. Sally was amazed by the number of men who wanted to dance with her.

Most of them were curious, of course. They wanted to know how she and Logan had met, and why they'd never run into her before. But while Sally found their sincere interest and praise flattering, she also found that the time dragged.

She was super-aware that Logan didn't dance. He remained among the bystanders, nursing a glass of red wine, chatting and watching from the sidelines. Waiting till his ordeal was over.

At last the music stopped and Diana Devenish, who must have been sequestered away in a corner, appeared on the edge of the dance floor beneath a spotlight.

Sally felt that same panicky dread she'd felt during exams when the teacher had said, 'You may commence reading your test paper…now.'

Logan, as the most generous donor, was to have the honour of dancing first. Any minute now, his name would be called out. Heart hammering, Sally made her way to his side. 'Just remember—' she began, but her throat was strangely parched and the rest of her sentence dried on her lips.

He smiled into her eyes. 'I'll remember. I'm a coat hanger. And I mustn't look down at my feet.'

She nodded and her throat was tight and sore. Logan's name was announced and she felt cold all over, sick with ridiculous nerves. He dipped his head, dropping a swift, warm kiss on her cool cheek.

'Break a leg,' she whispered.

'There's every chance,' came his dry reply and then he squared his shoulders and marched across the ballroom.

A subdued hush fell over the crowd as he approached Diana Devenish and Sally felt a cool hand clasp hers—Carissa was looking as nervous and sick as Sally felt.

'When he was a boy at school, he hated performing. Always got terrible stage fright,' Carissa whispered.

It was rather too late to be remembering that now, Sally

wanted to tell her. 'He'll be fine,' she said, but her stomach felt hollow and there was a scratchy soreness in her throat.

The attention of everyone in the room was focused on Diana Devenish and Logan.

'Mr Logan Black is the Managing Director of Blackcorp Mining Consultancies,' the MC told them. 'And he has chosen to dance the waltz with Ms Devenish.'

The lights in the ballroom dimmed and fine hairs lifted on Sally's arms as Logan entered the spotlight's circle with his shoulders back and his head proudly erect, as determined and brave as a gladiator entering the Colosseum.

Television cameras edged closer, zooming in as Diana Devenish greeted Logan with a kiss. Rising on tiptoe, she whispered something in his ear, smiled coyly and he nodded.

Then the band began to play a very lush and beautiful theme from a movie—a popular piece that everyone knew and loved. Logan took Diana's right hand in his and supported her back with his hand beneath her shoulder blade, just as Sally had taught him. *Think bra line.* Diana placed her left hand on his shoulder and smiled up at him, encouraging him to take the lead.

Logan didn't.

He didn't move. In fact, he looked as if his knees had locked and his feet were glued to the floor.

The music played on and Sally's throat squeezed tight. 'Just start counting,' she whispered, willing him to remember.

She knew that if Logan didn't move soon, Diana Devenish almost certainly would. Diana would probably drag him around the dance floor if she had to. But he would be mortified, would hate to admit defeat.

She tried to tell herself it didn't matter. Her emotional investment in Logan's success was foolish. This was only a dance, for heaven's sake. Nothing life-threatening. He would get over this embarrassment.

Easy to say…

Scared that she might actually cry, Sally closed her eyes and the lovely music continued, lilting and lush. One, two, three. One, two, three. *Can you count to three, Mr Black?*

She touched Chloe's locket. It seemed so silly now, to think of it as a good luck charm.

'Sally!' Carissa joggled her elbow. 'Sally, look!'

Forcing her eyes open, Sally felt her mouth wobble dangerously out of shape. Logan was dancing. He was leading with his body and gliding, gliding. Diana Devenish looked delighted as she floated in his arms, her high-heeled ruby shoes sparkling and twirling and her skirt trailing like a flame.

The handsome couple danced on and on, smoothly and elegantly, while the music swelled towards a dramatic conclusion and Logan, sensing that his ordeal was almost over, took Diana out into the centre and waltzed a little faster, showing off now. The crowd burst into applause and Sally, snuffling, clapped loudest of all.

It was ages before Logan was free. First he had to wait at Diana's table until the other two men had their turn at dancing. And then there were all kinds of strangers crowding in to offer their congratulations.

The whole time he was fielding their hugs and back slaps, he kept a weather eye open for Sally on the far side of the room where she was chatting to Carissa's friends. She looked, with her golden hair and her golden dress, like a slender beacon.

His little guiding light. If he hadn't already been in debt to Sally for saving his company, he was now. This evening he'd come within a hair's breadth of personal fiasco. He might have remained glued to the ballroom floor for ever if he hadn't heard her voice, whispering cheekily in his ear: *Can you count to three, Mr Black?*

After that, Diana Devenish and the crowd had disappeared. *One, two-three. Strong, soft-soft.* He'd been dancing with Sally in Blackcorp's boardroom with the tables and chairs shoved up against the walls. *The waltz is all about poise, grace and elegance.*

Thank you for everything, Sally Finch.

At last he reached her. She threw her arms around his neck and kissed him and told him that he was fabulous, as so many others had, but, for Logan, this embrace was nothing like the others. When he hugged Sally close, he wanted to pull her even closer and never let her go. She felt so absolutely right in his arms, as if she belonged there, clasped against his heart.

'I've been telling Sally she should open a dancing studio,' Carissa said when he finally, reluctantly, released Sally.

'She mustn't do that.' He looked down into Sally's shining eyes, as blue and bright as her topaz earrings. He touched his knuckles to her flushed cheek. 'I need her at Blackcorp.'

The colour mounted in Sally's cheeks. She gave her trademark warm, dazzling smile and a rocky lump wedged in Logan's throat. Last night's lovemaking had been beyond wonderful. Sally's exquisite tenderness, her emotional honesty and total lack of inhibition had set him craving more.

He'd never felt desire with this deep intensity and he'd give anything to be able to whisk her away from here. Now. He would take her back to his place. Or hers. Anywhere where they could be together. Alone.

'I think it must be my turn to dance with you, Sally.' Geoff's voice broke into Logan's distracted thoughts.

Sally turned to Carissa's husband and beamed at him. 'I'd love that, Geoff. And hey, it's a tango! Let's go!'

They hurried away like happy children, hand in hand, laughing even before they reached the dance floor. Jealously,

Logan watched as they began to dance, grinning madly as they tangoed across the room, arms extended and cheeks touching.

Sally was so lovely, such fun. Everyone who met her was charmed by her vibrancy and warmth. She was like a tonic enriching his life.

As if she knew what he was thinking, Sally turned on the dance floor and looked back over her shoulder at him. Her eyes sparkled as their eyes met and she sent him a smile shining with love.

And then he knew...with unsettling clarity...that Sally had fallen in love with him. If only he was free to love her. If only…

Hell.

An ominous, deathlike clamp gripped his heart and he almost cried out in pain. He'd made a terrible, unforgivable mistake.

Last night Sally had told him about the rat who'd attacked her and he'd felt so protective. He'd wanted to shield her from the world.

But how could he? How could he stick to his five-year plan and remain on the pedestal she'd placed him on?

Last night she'd said: *Isn't honesty the best thing?*

That had been his cue.

He should have told her then. *While we're being honest, sweetheart, I have this business plan, which doesn't, unfortunately, allow me the luxury of a romance.*

But if he'd told her that he would have ruined a beautiful, utterly perfect moment.

Sins of omission can be the most dangerous.

Hattie had told him that. And the really terrible thing was he'd been so damn eager to have another bout of fabulous sex with Sally that he'd avoided telling her an important detail—that his emotions were on hold for another five years.

Actually, he should have made sure she understood that *before* he'd lured her into his bed. He'd totally ignored his vow to keep his distance from Sally Finch. He'd known from the start that she wasn't a sophisticated city woman, but a sweet country girl who believed in falling in love, in two people becoming soul mates and living happy-ever-after.

Which made him as bad as that creep who'd attacked her at the dance. And what was his excuse? That he'd been floating high yesterday because Sally had saved his company? Pumped with euphoria, overflowing with gratitude? How honourable was that?

Last night's emotions did not excuse him from giving in to forbidden desires. He should have remembered that, no matter how desperately he wanted Sally, he could not give her the emotional commitment she needed and deserved.

He should have been honest. Sally had told him about that rat because she trusted him. Poor darling. She'd trusted a man who hadn't the fortitude to tell her there was no space on his agenda for love.

But how would he find the strength to give her up?

Groaning heavily, Logan looked down at the drink someone had thrust in his hand. He had no choice. He had to be honest, had to tell Sally that he wasn't in a position to commit.

Carissa came to stand beside him and gave him a nudge with her elbow as she cocked her head in Sally's direction. 'Tell me, little brother, are you still stuck on your crazy five-year plan?'

'Of course,' he hissed through gritted teeth.

Carissa's mouth flattened unhappily as she watched Sally. 'That poor girl.' She turned and shook her head at him. 'Five years. That's sixty months. It's ridiculous.'

Logan tried to ignore the sickening hollow in his chest. He feared Carissa was right, but he couldn't change his plans. Yesterday's close encounter with financial disaster had proved that. In five years' time, if all went well, his business would be secure enough for him to relax, to look around and find a life partner. Until then, he had to put his emotional life on hold.

God help him, Sally deserved the truth.

CHAPTER THIRTEEN

THE sore throat that had started while Sally was watching Logan dance with Diana Devenish got worse on the way home. It was raining again, pelting at the car windows and rushing along the gutters, adding a sinister touch to the midnight journey.

Sally was exhausted, but that was what you got when you danced till you dropped.

'Tired?' Logan asked as the car zipped past a crowd getting soaked as they came out of a nightclub.

'No, not tired at all,' she lied.

Actually, her limbs were aching and her head had begun to throb in time with the back and forth action of the windscreen wipers. It couldn't be a hangover. She'd been too busy dancing and had hardly touched her champagne.

Whatever the cause, she wasn't going to pay any attention to her aches. No way could she let them spoil this fabulous night.

This perfect night.

Logan drove on in silence, but for Sally it was a comfortable silence. Curled languorously with her cheek against the soft leather upholstery, she stared out into the slanting rain and decided that *perfect* was the only word to describe this evening. Nothing had marred the Hospital Ball's dazzling brilliance.

She'd worn a spectacular gown. Logan had been dreamily handsome and a flatteringly attentive partner. Carissa and Geoff had made her feel completely at ease. And she'd danced with countless good-looking guys, all apparently rolling in money. To cap it off, the dancing lessons, that she'd fretted over, couldn't have turned in better results.

With a faraway smile, she rubbed Chloe's locket. The talisman had worked its magic and her godmother would have been proud of her. Come to think of it, her parents and brothers would have been proud, too. The menacing shadows of the past were vanquished. She was a new woman.

Any way Sally looked at it, her decision to come to Sydney had been the right one.

Logan pulled up outside her house and she felt a leap of happy anticipation. It was about to happen. The perfect ending to this perfect night. Best case scenario, she'd be with Logan till dawn. And the only improvement on that would be spending the rest of her life with him. She'd fallen so deeply in love with this man that she feared there was no way back.

'Well,' she said, in a what-happens-next voice, 'thanks for a wonderful evening, Logan.'

He turned off the ignition and released his seat belt. 'I have to thank *you*, Sally. For everything.' He leaned towards her and touched her cheek with the knuckle of his forefinger. 'I owe you so much.'

Something about his manner—an edge of carefulness and formality—bothered her. Where was last night's easy banter? Where were his ready smiles? His passion? They were alone, for heaven's sake. Why wasn't she in Logan's arms?

All night she'd seen the hunger in his eyes; she'd felt the heat of his longing whenever he'd touched her. But now she could only sense a new distance between them. A frightening distance.

She hunted for something light to say. 'Now I can boast that I've danced with the man who's danced with Diana Devenish.'

He gave a half-hearted chuckle.

'I'm so proud of you, Logan.'

'The credit's all yours, Sally.'

She shook her head. 'You were very brave. Carissa told me you used to get stage fright.'

'Carissa has too much to say.'

He looked worried as he said this and he sighed heavily. Desperate to avoid ending this fabulous night on such an unsatisfactory note, Sally said quickly, 'Would you like to come in for coffee?'

His eyes flashed. 'Thanks, I'd like that.'

Phew. Thank heavens he wasn't running away. Sally told herself she'd been worrying about nothing.

'There should be an umbrella,' he said, peering into the gloom of the back seat. 'Yes, here it is. Wait there. We don't want to get your lovely dress wet.'

The rain was gusting strongly when Logan opened Sally's door and he tried to shield her with the umbrella as well as his body. She gathered up her long skirt to keep it clear of puddles, slipped off her strappy gold shoes, and they ran together through the rain to her front door.

Breathless, she fumbled in her clutch bag for her key while Logan closed the umbrella and set it in a corner of the porch.

The door swung open and he followed her inside. Sally switched on the light in the front hallway and she turned to him expectantly. *Now* he would haul her into his lovely strong arms.

But no.

Logan stood stiffly, hands tightly clenched at his sides. His jaw was clenched too, and his dark eyes held frightening shadows. He gave the slightest shake of his head, as if to warn her gently of impending danger, and fear strafed through her like a deadly bullet.

'I was hoping we could talk,' he said.

Talk? Not even a kiss? After last night's incredible passion? After the glamour and romance of the ball?

Sally needed to close her eyes as she adjusted to this. What did Logan want to talk about? Surely it could only be bad news.

Was he going to tell her that last night had been an aberration—a celebratory fling after the shock of almost losing his company? But what about the ball? Would he feel compelled to remind her that it had been no more than a charity commitment? Was it back to business as usual for the boss of Blackcorp and the front desk girl?

Fighting disappointment, Sally tried to think straight, took a steadying breath. 'The kitchen's this way.'

Logan followed her through to the cosy, bright kitchen. He took off his jacket, which had damp patches on the shoulders, and hung it on the back of a chair. In his white shirt and bow-tie, he seemed somehow bigger and Sally had to remember to breathe as she filled the kettle.

'Tea or coffee?' she asked. 'I prefer tea at this time of night.'

'So do I.'

See, we're compatible, she wanted to joke, but this was no longer a night for joking. While the water came to the boil, Logan leaned casually against the door of the fridge and she tried to look busy, getting the teapot and a tea strainer, mugs and sugar and a tin of shortbread.

'I'll need milk,' she said over her shoulder. 'If you could get it out of the fridge, please.'

When their mugs were filled with tea—black with two sugars for Logan, white with one for Sally—she suggested they go through to the lounge room.

'I'd prefer to stay here,' Logan said, looking distinctly uncomfortable.

Oh, yes. The lounge room held untold dangers. The sofa, for instance.

'Take a seat, then,' she said, pulling out a chair for herself. She thought how incongruous they must look, sitting at a scrubbed pine kitchen table in their glamorous evening finery, sipping tea like an old married couple.

Don't even think that word.

Unwillingly, she asked, 'What did you want to talk about?'

Logan's mouth turned down and he stared at the pattern on the side of his mug. 'We've had two wonderful evenings,' he said and then he paused and looked uncomfortable.

Oh, help. This was terrible.

'But you don't want me to get the wrong idea,' Sally said quietly.

He grimaced and looked more uncomfortable than ever. 'There's something I should have told you, Sally.'

A cold chill gripped her stomach. 'There's someone else?'

'No, of course not.'

'You're not secretly engaged, or anything like that?'

'Nothing like that.'

Sally waited.

'But I should have warned you that I'm totally committed to my business and I will be for some time. I can't afford any kind of emotional attachments. I've put my personal life on hold.'

'Really? How long will it be on hold?'

'For another five years,' he said.

This sounded ridiculous to Sally. 'So last night was the last time you'll make love for five years? Get serious, Logan.'

He looked embarrassed. 'That's not what I meant.'

'But you're telling me that you're not even open for a casual relationship.'

His eyes registered surprise and he seemed to have to think about this before he replied. He sighed heavily. 'You're not that kind of girl.'

No, she wasn't, but this was a battle and she was a fighter. 'You don't know what kind of girl I am.'

'I know enough to be sure I'm not right for you. You'd end up getting hurt, Sally, and I'd hate that. That's why I think it would be wise if we took a step back from each other. Put everything back on a business footing.'

How could he be so calm about this? Hadn't last night meant anything? *Damn him.* He was as bad as her bossy brothers, deciding whose emotions he was going to protect and whose he was going to stuff up. 'If you're trying to protect me, don't bother. I don't need it.'

Logan's attempt at a smile failed. He looked unhappily at his mug and fiddled with the handle.

Sally found it hard to keep anger from her voice. 'Just for the record, Logan, I wasn't expecting you to get down on your knees tonight and offer a proposal of marriage.'

'I'm sorry,' he said gruffly. 'I've offended you.'

'I'm tougher than you think.'

Warmth crept into his eyes and the skin around them creased sexily.

Unfair. Why did he have to look so attractive when he was busily rejecting her? 'I think you owe me a better explanation,' she said but, before he could reply, she remembered, with a sharp pang of dismay, her last conversation with Hattie. She groaned.

Logan sent her a wary glance.

'Your grandmother warned me that this was likely to happen.'

'I'm cursed with a family of interfering women.'

Sally couldn't let him get away with that. 'Hattie and Carissa are wonderful. I really like them. And I'm sure your mother must be nice too.'

'She's very nice. But at least she's safely out of the way at the moment—caravanning around Australia.'

'Hattie told me that too.' His parents were travelling together. And Hattie had also mentioned that Logan was funding their travel. Did he have an urge to manage and protect everyone? Hattie? His parents? Her?

'Did Hattie also tell you about my father's bankruptcy?'

'No.' But Sally realised that it must be significant. Logan had mentioned a family bankruptcy yesterday and he'd indicated his fear of it happening again.

'My father had no real head for business,' he said. 'He gambled on the most reckless schemes. Our family lost everything.'

'Was that when you had to leave your private school?' she asked, remembering what he'd told her at the team-building workshop.

'Yes, but I coped.' His face was stony. 'My father didn't. He had a nervous breakdown and couldn't work again. My mother had to go out to work just to feed us.'

'And you've never forgiven your father,' Sally said quietly. She wanted to cry. How could Logan let his father's mistakes rule his life?

'It's not so much a matter of forgiveness.' Logan's jaw jutted stubbornly. 'I learned a valuable lesson about planning for the future. I have to make absolutely certain that my finances are completely secure before I consider marriage or a family. I won't be looking for a permanent relationship for at least five years.'

'What happens then?' This time Sally didn't even try to hold back her anger. 'Will you take a quick look around and find Miss Right just sitting there, waiting to be snapped up?'

'It's not as simplistic as it sounds.'

'It's worse, Logan.' He was looking stubborn and gorgeous in equal parts and Sally wanted to hit him. She couldn't stop thinking about the way he'd made love to her. How could he have been so tender and beautiful with her, so intense and passionate and then walk away as if it meant nothing?

Why couldn't he see that emotional well-being was equally if not more important than financial security?

'Tell me,' she demanded hotly, 'what will you do if you fall in love with someone before the five years are up?'

He shook his head. 'That won't happen.'

'How can you be so sure?'

'I won't allow it to happen.'

'You're crazy!' Something inside Sally snapped. She thumped her mug on the table and leapt to her feet. Tears clogged her throat as she raised her voice. 'In another five years you might grow up.'

'Sally!' Logan was on his feet too. 'I didn't want to upset you.'

'I'm not upset.' They both knew it was a lie, but she wasn't about to admit that she was angry, that she felt used, that her heart was ripping itself into a thousand pieces.

'I suppose you'd like me to leave,' he said quietly.

No, no! She wanted to plead with him to stay and it almost killed her to be strong. She said icily, 'You've made it obvious there's no reason for you to stay. I'm sure you have a business to worry about!'

Grim-faced, Logan picked up his damp jacket and shrugged into it.

They didn't speak as they walked to the door. This was unbearable. Logan's hang-ups had ruined everything. Sally was sure he had strong feelings for her. They should have been taking up where they'd left off last night—like any normal couple who were madly attracted to each other. But he'd chosen to punish himself and punish her as well. How dared he play with her emotions?

They reached the front hallway. 'Sally, you're a wonderful—'

'Don't!' she shouted as her disappointment and anger exploded. 'You've said enough.' Fighting tears, she reached behind and slid down the zip on her dress.

'What are you doing?'

She glared at him. 'Giving you back the dress you paid so much precious money for.' She pushed the straps aside and wriggled her shoulders free.

'B-but you don't have to.'

'I most certainly do. And you know it!' The dress slid downwards in a silken whisper.

Logan gaped at her. He looked as if he were about to burst a blood vessel.

Wearing nothing but her strapless bra and tiny panties, she stepped haughtily out of the golden pool of fabric, then scooped it up and thrust it into his hands. 'Thanks a million, Mr Black. I adored wearing this.'

She opened the door for him, but Logan was too stunned to move, so she set her hands squarely in his midriff and pushed him. He got the message then and backed away with the rippling gold gown in his hands.

The last thing Sally saw was the pain and sad loss in his eyes. She had just enough time to slam the door before she burst into tears.

CHAPTER FOURTEEN

UPSTAIRS in her bedroom, Sally threw herself on to the rose satin quilt and gave way to a bitter storm of weeping. She was so disillusioned, so mad with herself. She'd stupidly—*stupidly*—allowed herself to fall heart and soul for a man who had no capacity for returning her love.

Last night, the most beautiful night of her life, she'd given Logan everything. *Everything.* They'd been so close. He'd shared his lovely fantasy—Brahms, wine, the red couch—and she was sure he'd felt true emotional connection, so much more than lust.

And she'd bared her soul to him, had told him he'd healed her of her fear.

How naïve she'd been. Now she knew there were many ways to be hurt. She couldn't bear that Logan wasn't in love with her. But that was the truth. Logan was only interested in her skills as a receptionist and as a dancing instructor and to-night, the second most wonderful night of her life, she'd been left with nothing but humiliation and heartbreak.

When she'd finished crying about that, Sally cried for Chloe, who had wanted her to be so happy here in Sydney, and she cried for Hattie, who had warned her about her grand-son, but who'd also given her reason to hope.

Vain hope.

Sally's throat, already sore before the tears had begun, ached unbearably now. And she was cold as she lay on top of the bed in her scanty underwear, but she stayed there for ages, shivering and racked by sobbing, too utterly miserable to climb sensibly under the covers.

It was a long time before her exhaustion and the cold stilled her tears. When she sat up, her head ached horribly. She ached all over and she thought, for an awful moment, that she might throw up. Dragging Chloe's blue kimono about her, she staggered through to the bathroom to wash her face.

Her reflection in the mirror was shocking. Even after she'd washed away the black streaks of mascara, her eyes were red and puffy and her face was white with dark red blotches. Her hair was a mess of curls matted with hairspray and the blue topaz earrings winked in the mirror, mocking her. She remembered how happy and excited she'd been when she'd put them on and almost started crying again.

Back in her bedroom, she carefully removed the earrings and put them in the velvet-lined box. She undid the locket, felt again the cool, solid weight of it in her hands and turned it over, wondering about the times her godmother had worn this jewellery. She hoped they'd been happier times than tonight.

And, as she climbed beneath the bedclothes, it occurred to her that she wasn't really like Chloe at all. In her bid for independence, she'd been trying to live Chloe's life, but now that she'd fallen helplessly in love, Sally understood that it wasn't living in a big city or living the high life that made a person happy. Building a life together with the one special person you loved was the secret to happiness.

But Logan had a very different vision and he was so focused on his goal that he wouldn't recognise a chance for lifelong happiness if it kissed him on the lips.

Or taught him to waltz.

Logan fretted and fumed as he paced the white-carpeted length of his penthouse. If ever a man deserved a booby prize for blunders, he did. From the day he'd first seen Sally Finch he'd made stuff-up after stuff-up.

His frantic gaze flashed to her gown, now lying where he'd flung it, a river of gold flowing over the red sofa. He pictured Sally as he'd seen her last, standing before him like an avenging angel, with her head proudly high, her eyes shooting daggers while she looked utterly divine in her wispy, barely-there underwear. Before she'd sent him packing.

In spite of his self-loathing, Logan's mouth twisted in a wry half smile. What spunk Sally had! He was full of admiration for her. She was gutsy and warm-hearted, loyal and kind, clever and sexy—the list could go on and on.

In a word, she was perfect.

And he'd rejected her out of hand.

Tonight, she'd asked: *What will you do if you fall in love with someone before the five years are up?*

And he'd told her in all seriousness: *That won't happen.*

Fool! What a simpleton he was. An idiot. An arrogant, totally unthinking moron who'd flirted with an innocent, courageous and perfect girl, and then thoughtlessly seduced her and toyed with her emotions. Had toyed, unthinkingly, with his own emotions as well.

Realising this, Logan remembered the challenge in Sally's eyes.

You've never forgiven your father.

At the time he'd brushed her comment aside. He'd been too tense to stop, to give her accusation any consideration. But was Sally right? Did he hold a long-term grudge against his father? Had he allowed it to sour his life? He feared Carissa would agree. And perhaps his mother would too, even though she'd borne the brunt of his father's failure.

Never once had his mother's love faltered. She'd forgiven her husband for all the hardship he'd brought on her. She still adored the man she'd married.

Logan's throat closed over a tight knot of pain. His parents were having the most wonderful time, travelling around Australia together in their little caravan. In spite of everything, life had always been an adventure for his mother.

Sally would see life as an adventure too. Not as an endurance test, not as one long, dangerous minefield poised to detonate beneath her feet.

Through the plate glass window that faced the east, he saw glimmering pink threads of dawn. He thought about the sun rising and setting on his life, over and over for the next five years until he was free to throw off his chains and embrace his future.

Carissa had reminded him that five years amounted to sixty months. It was close on two *thousand* days.

A hell of a lot of dawns. Two thousand pink dawns and fiery sunsets.

Two thousand velvet-black nights which, thanks to his foolproof five-year plan, he would spend minus Sally.

He had a lot of thinking to do.

The sound of knocking penetrated Sally's sleep and she supposed she should try to wake up. She opened one eye tentatively and knew immediately that she was ill. Her head throbbed, her throat was on fire and every inch of her body ached. She was aware of sunlight blazing behind her floral curtains, but she had no idea what time it was.

Had someone really been knocking? Perhaps she'd dreamed it. It didn't really matter because there was no way she could get downstairs to open the door. She needed all her strength to reach for the glass on her bedside table and take a sip of water, couldn't imagine how she would make it to the bathroom.

As the water forced its painful way down her throat, she remembered that Logan didn't love her. She remembered everything—his five-year plan, her anger and embarrassment, taking off the dress and flinging it at him and slamming the door. Fiery tears seeped beneath her eyelids and burned down her cheeks. She buried her head in the pillow and told herself to forget about her boss or she might never recover.

She needed to sleep. Needed to sleep for a week.

The next time Sally woke, the telephone was ringing downstairs. There were long shadows in the room, so she decided that it must be late afternoon. Chloe had never had the phone connected upstairs and Sally's automatic response was to try to get out of bed to answer it, but she was hit by a wave of dizziness and sank back on to the pillows again.

Who could be calling? She had no choice but to lie helplessly and listen to the shrill bell below, ringing on and on.

It was dark the next time the phone woke her. She didn't make it downstairs in time, but she went on shaky legs to the bathroom, found some aspirin and replenished her glass of water, crawled back into bed again.

She had only just settled when her mobile phone on the bedside table rang. Blindly, she groped for it. 'Hello.'

'Sally, it's Anna.'

'Oh, Anna. Hi.'

'What's the matter with you? You sound awful.'

'I'm sick. I think I must have the flu.'

'Ooh, that's terrible.' There was a pause. 'I was ringing to see if you'd like to come for lunch tomorrow.'

'Sorry. Too sick.'

'You poor thing. Do you need anything? How are you off for food?'

'I don't need anything. I'm not hungry.'

'You sound as if you need looking after.'

'No.' Sally shook her head and winced when it hurt. 'Don't worry about me. I'd hate you to catch this.'

'I must admit I wouldn't want to give the flu to Oliver.'

'No, I'll be all right. I just need to sleep.'

'Make sure you take plenty of fluids.'

'Yup.'

'What a waste of a weekend, though,' Anna said before she rang off.

There was one distinct advantage to sleeping all weekend, Sally decided as she drifted off again. She couldn't think too much about Logan.

The weekend was the most frustrating Logan had ever known. As far as he could tell, Sally had gone away for the entire two days, leaving him to endure hours and hours and *hours* in gloomy solitude.

But if he thought the weekend was bad, Monday morning was worse. It began with Sally's conspicuous absence from the front desk and went rapidly downhill from there.

Everyone at Blackcorp had either seen him dancing with Diana Devenish on television, or had heard about it, and he was showered with congratulations and questions, especially about Sally's involvement. Logan did his best to defend Sally and his choice of her as his dancing instructor, but it was all rather embarrassing and difficult.

Coming on top of Maria Paige's departure, the possibility

that he and Sally might be in a relationship would send the gossips at the water-cooler into a total frenzy.

Of course, everyone expected him to know why Sally wasn't at work today. He had no idea, but her absence worried him. *Really* worried him.

He was in Janet Keaton's office, where he was firming up strategies for securing Maria's replacement, when he learned that Sally had phoned in sick.

'Sick?' The possibility had never occurred to Logan. He needed to loosen his shirt collar, which was suddenly way too tight. Sweat broke out on his brow. Was Sally honestly sick? Or was she avoiding him?

'When did this happen?' he asked Janet.

'Sally's been sick all weekend, apparently. With the flu.'

He couldn't bear to think that was true. He'd spent hours over the weekend staring at the drawn curtains over Sally's windows. Surely she hadn't been lying inside the house all that time?

'I thought you must have known,' Janet said. 'Sally spent Friday night at the Hospital Ball with you, didn't she?'

'She did.' Logan frowned. 'And she was perfectly well then.'

'I've heard on the grapevine that she taught you to waltz.'

Logan's response was a distracted nod. He was picturing Sally, lying helpless and alone in that house, behind those drawn curtains, all weekend, too ill to answer the door or come to the phone. The poor girl.

He charged out of the office.

'Logan,' Janet called after him, 'don't run off just yet. There's something I've been meaning to ask you.'

An annoyed sigh escaped him and he hovered in the doorway, one impatient hand on the frame, ready to launch out of there. 'What is it?'

With infuriating calm, Janet left her chair and came to stand next to him. Arms folded comfortably, she slid him a shrewd sideways glance. 'Am I right in guessing that my blind date strategy grew into something bigger?'

'What blind date? What are you talking about?'

'At the team-building workshop. When I paired you with Sally.'

Puzzled, he shook his head. So much had happened since that workshop, he'd almost forgotten it. But it was the first occasion he and Sally had spent time together. He'd told her then that he couldn't dance and everything else had unfolded from there.

If they hadn't been paired off, none of the rest would have happened. He'd be free of this torment now. But he would have missed the joy of knowing Sally, the bliss of making love to her.

Janet's eyes lost their amused sparkle. In all seriousness, she said, 'I knew you and Sally would be good for each other.'

Logan's chest squeezed so tightly it hurt him to breathe. 'How did you work that out?'

'I've seen your personality profiles.' Janet spoke as if the answer was obvious. 'Sally's an extroverted feeling type, which means she's tactful, friendly, but a little too sensitive. And you're an introverted thinker. You're logical and organised, but disinclined to trust your instincts.'

Instincts?

His instincts had been leading him a merry dance ever since that first time he'd met Sally after the baby had crawled under his desk.

Logan shook his head. 'What's the point of these personality profiles? What do they prove?'

'That you and Sally complement each other perfectly.'

To his surprise, Logan found this idea incredibly cheering and he realised suddenly that he was grinning. Quickly, he looked away, making an embarrassed, throat-clearing sound. 'Right…well…er…I know there are other matters we need to discuss, Janet, but I'm afraid we'll have to deal with them later.'

Without looking back to see her reaction, Logan hurried away.

Sally could hear noises coming from downstairs in the kitchen.

She sat up quickly, clutching at the bed sheets and pulling them up to her chin as she listened to footsteps on the tiles, a cupboard door squeaking on its hinge and something banging against a pot. Her heart began a frantic canter. She had been feeling much stronger this morning. She'd had a bath and washed her hair and put fresh linen on her bed, but she was still too feeble to deal with an intruder.

'Who's there?' Her cry was so weak she was quite sure it wouldn't carry all the way downstairs. Perhaps, if she remained very quiet, the burglar would help himself to whatever he wanted and leave.

No. That wasn't going to happen. The footsteps were coming up the stairs. *Oh, help!*

She scanned her bedroom quickly, wondering what on earth she could use as a weapon. She'd intended to go to self-defence classes when she came to Sydney, but she hadn't got around to it yet. Memories of that night with Kyle Francis at the ball filled her head. Those vile masculine hands constraining her, that brutish, repugnant body forcing her down…

Could she escape? Hide under the bed?

'Sally, don't be frightened. It's only me.'

That was Logan's voice.

Was it really him? Her heart took off like a rocket. How could Logan be here? She felt too shocked to respond. Her hands flew to her hair. She looked terrible! Logan mustn't see her like this.

But it was too late to get tidy—he was already in her

bedroom doorway. And, despite her misery over everything that had happened between them, she feasted her eyes on him and felt a rush of mad joy, swiftly followed by a cold splash of sanity. And then an ache that settled in the hollow around her heart.

Logan was dressed for work in his usual dark business suit, but there were dusty white smudges on his jacket sleeves and his trousers. His shirt collar was undone and the knot of his tie was skewed to a rakish angle, making him look less like a businessman and more like a film star. A terribly worried film star.

'Hi there,' he said, smiling shyly.

'Hello.'

What did you say to a lover you'd thrown out three nights ago?

Sally tried again. 'How did you get in?'

'I climbed over your back wall.'

Good heavens. That explained the smudges of whitewash on his clothes. But why on earth had he gone to so much trouble?

Uncomfortably self-conscious and confused, Sally tugged the bed sheet closer to her neck. 'What—what are you doing here?'

It was an important question, but Logan ignored it. 'How are you, Sally?'

'Great.'

He frowned at her. 'Come on, be truthful.'

'Well, I'm alive.'

'You look pale.'

'You get that with the flu. Why aren't you at work?'

'I heard you were sick. I had to come.'

He *had* to come? She felt tears threaten and hoped she didn't cry. 'I suppose everyone's talking about us after Friday night.'

'Let them talk.' He came into the room, crossing the floor all the way to her bed, and Sally feared she might hyperventilate.

'You'll get my germs,' she felt compelled to warn him.

Ignoring her again, Logan sat on the edge of her bed and frowned thoughtfully as he placed his hand on her forehead.

Sally flinched at his touch and he flushed, took his hand away quickly and frowned more deeply. 'Have you been eating?'

'Not much.' Yesterday she'd crawled downstairs and found a packet of dry crackers and a two litre carton of orange juice. 'I haven't been very hungry.'

'I've brought you some chicken soup. It's heating on the stove.'

But why? Nothing about this made sense. Logan had thrown her out of his life and she'd thrown him out of her home and now he was fussing in her kitchen like a nursemaid.

'That's very kind of you, Logan.'

His dark eyes glowed and he smiled sternly. 'Don't go away. I'll be back in a minute.'

Heart thumping madly, Sally listened to his footsteps as he went back down the stairs. She heard the sounds of pots and crockery being moved about in the kitchen. She felt light-headed with unexplained happiness and told herself that was *not* sensible. Logan hadn't come here to make her happy. He was in protection mode. He was overriding Friday night's unceremonious eviction and he'd come to boss her around.

Just the same, it was wonderful to see him.

He was back as quickly as he'd promised, bearing a wooden tray with a large white bowl filled with soup, a silver soup spoon and a pink gingham napkin, all of which he must have found in her kitchen. He put everything on her dressing table, came to her bedside again and smiled down at her. 'Let's rearrange these pillows so you can sit up comfortably.'

It had to be the flu that made her so dreadfully tearful. She couldn't bear Logan's kindness, but she mustn't cry. As he fetched her tray, she swiped at her eyes and drew in a long, deep, steadying breath, then let it out very slowly.

'Now—' he sat on the edge of her bed, far too close to her, and his dark eyes were heartbreakingly gorgeous as he lifted a spoonful of soup to her lips '—try some of this.'

Sally protested, 'I don't expect you to feed me.' But she knew her hands were shaking and she couldn't manage the soup without spilling it on the bedclothes.

Logan tilted a spoonful into her mouth. The soup was light and delicious and slipped down easily. It tasted wholesome and nourishing and Sally quickly found that she was starving.

He fed her carefully and patiently, with the tenderest smile in his lovely dark eyes.

'This is wonderful,' she said between mouthfuls. 'It doesn't taste like soup out of a can.'

'That's possibly because it's not soup out of a can.'

'Did your housekeeper make it?'

He shook his head and smiled. 'I woke Michel.'

'Your chef friend? You woke him? Logan, you shouldn't have.'

He shrugged. 'It was high time he got up.'

'But he works long hours at night.'

'Stop fretting, Sally. Once I explained that it was *you* who needed this soup, Michel couldn't have been more helpful. We both have videophones, so he was able to give me step by step instructions without setting a toe out of bed.'

'So you made this soup?' Her voice echoed her surprise.

He tried to shrug nonchalantly, but Sally could see that he was rather proud of his efforts. She ate some more, enjoying succulent pieces of chicken, carrot and celery and light traces of herbs. 'I feel as if I'm getting better already.'

It wasn't quite true. She actually felt dizzy. She had no idea why Logan was being so kind. He'd told her once that he never made romantic gestures, but didn't he understand that his kindness now was more touching, more upsetting than any bouquet of roses?

Tears threatened to spill again, but she ate her way stolidly to the bottom of the bowl. Logan took the tray and set it back on the dressing table.

'There's plenty more,' he said as he returned once again to sit on the edge of her bed.

'I couldn't eat any more just now, but thank you so much for that. You'll pass on my thanks to Michel, won't you?'

He nodded and reached for her hands, enclosing them in his. Her impulse was to pull them away. She and Logan had broken up. But something about the soft light in his eyes prevented her from moving.

He said, 'Michel was over-the-top excited about your soup.'

'Really? Why?'

'You know what he's like. When he realised I was taking food to your sick bed, he started rattling on about catering for my wedding.'

Zap! Sally's poor heart almost shot out of the window. She felt the sudden threat of tears and she squeezed her eyes tightly shut to hold them back. 'What a weird thing to say.'

'Not so very weird. Just romantic.'

'I suppose Michel knows he's going to have to wait five years? At least he'll have plenty of time to refine the menu.'

'Perhaps not.'

Was she delirious?

Not daring to open her eyes, Sally sank back against the pillows and lay very still. Her head was fuzzy and she knew she was terribly confused. Why was Logan talking about weddings and caterers who didn't have to wait and—?

'Sally, look at me.'

No. She couldn't. If she opened her eyes, her tears might spill and she couldn't bear that humiliation.

'Sally, darling.'

Darling? Her eyes shot open.

Logan's smile was terribly worried and his eyes were shining with a suspicious dampness. He swallowed. 'I want you to know that acting on the best advice available, I've binned the five-year plan.'

'Who—' Sally swallowed to get rid of the strangled feeling in her throat '—who told you to do that?'

'A little bird pointed out some important home truths.'

'I don't understand. What are you saying?'

'A very brave little golden Finch pointed out that I was an ostrich with my head in the sand, avoiding the truth.'

'The truth?'

'Yes, the truth that you, Sally, are without question the most wonderful woman I have ever met and I can't imagine trying to face life without you.'

Miraculously, all at once, the hollow pain around her heart began to ease.

'I should have told you this on Friday night after the ball,' Logan said, 'but I stuffed up and did the exact opposite.'

The mere mention of that terrible night made her shudder. 'I didn't help. I threw you out.'

'I deserved it, Sally. I thought I was being honest with you, protecting you. But I was being totally dishonest about how I really feel. When I was standing out on the street, I knew that I was losing you and I couldn't bear it.'

Yes, she'd seen the loss in his eyes and it had nearly killed her.

'It was the worst night of my life,' Logan said.

'Mine, too.'

'I came around early the next day and knocked on your

door. I telephoned a couple of times. I drove past your house countless times, but there were no signs of life, so I assumed you'd taken off for the weekend. I was petrified when you didn't turn up at work this morning. I was sure I'd lost you.'

'Poor thing.' Reaching up, Sally touched his face with her fingertips, savoured the masculine rasp of the skin on his jaw. 'There's no need to look so worried.'

He smiled crookedly, then drew her into his arms and kissed her beautifully.

'I hope I don't give you the flu.'

His lips were warm as he nuzzled her neck just below her ear. 'If I catch the flu, you can look after me.'

'I'd love to.'

He kissed her again. And again.

And again.

EPILOGUE

WITH his white shirtsleeves rolled up and a long apron loosely tied about his hips, Logan stood at the stove in Sally's kitchen and stirred a mint sauce while he kept an eye on steaming peas. He'd taken quite a liking to this cooking caper.

A wintry wind whistled outside, knocking at the windows and buffeting the doors, and he hoped the forecast rain held off until their guests arrived and were safely inside. Hattie, Carissa and Geoff, Sally's brother, Steve, and his wife were all due any minute now.

Everything was ready. Sally had set the table in the dining room with the best silver and china and she'd done clever things with flowers and candles so that the room looked enchanting and perfect for their first dinner party.

Now she was upstairs, touching up her lipstick and tidying her hair. For a wistful moment Logan pictured her up there, applying colour to her soft lips, tweaking a golden curl, spraying scent on her wrists and her cleavage.

He closed his eyes as desire pounded through him. *Easy, man. Keep your mind in the kitchen.*

Here in the kitchen, the air was warm and fragrant with the scent of roasting lamb and rosemary and sizzling potatoes. Copper-shaded lights warmed the whitewashed walls and terracotta tiles and picked up the honeyed tones of the timber cupboards. With the wind roaring outside, everything in this room looked especially cosy tonight.

Logan was glad that he and Sally had finally decided to live here rather than in his penthouse. They'd spent the past six months dividing their time between both places and it had been fun for a while, but it was good to be settled.

He liked the sense of permanence the decision had brought. Besides, Sally was very emotionally attached to this house and they were renting out his penthouse for an outrageous sum.

Everything was working out amazingly well. In spite of ditching his five-year plan, his business was going from strength to strength. He'd tried to coax Sally into taking his PA's position, but she'd vetoed that idea. In the end, he'd known she was wise to leave Blackcorp and get a new job in Chloe's favourite art gallery.

Now, they both shared an interest in his business but, at the end of the working day, they came to each other as lovers rather than co-workers.

Life with Sally was, as Logan had always suspected, incredibly romantic and an enormous adventure.

'Oh, no! That apron has to go. It makes you look far too sexy.'

At the sound of Sally's voice Logan spun around. She was wearing a cream silk blouse with black velvet trousers and she'd done something with her hair to make it look sophisticated, yet casual and utterly gorgeous.

He grinned at her. 'You look good enough to eat.'

'I'm afraid fiancées aren't on the menu tonight.' She smiled as she waved her left hand at him, making the solitaire diamond flash and sparkle. 'Just roast lamb, followed by poached pears with Mascarpone.'

'But I can have you for hors d'oeuvres.'

'Of course you can.' Laughing, she crossed the kitchen and wound her arms about his neck. Her slender curves pressed close and she touched her lips to his jaw and a soft groan escaped him. Maybe this wasn't such a great idea after all. With Sally in his arms, he feared he'd be in no fit state to greet their guests.

'I hope they don't stay too late tonight,' she said, grinning cheekily. 'I can't wait to tell our families the wonderful news about our wedding, but by the end of this evening I'll be desperate to be alone with you.'

They shared a smile, a private and intimate smile, brimming with promise, and Logan gathered her close again.

Two nights ago, right here in this kitchen, this wonderful woman had agreed to marry him. Now he created havoc with her lipstick just as the front doorbell rang.

* * * * *

Here is a sneak preview of
A STONE CREEK CHRISTMAS,
the latest in Linda Lael Miller's acclaimed
McKETTRICK *series.*

A lonely horse brought vet Olivia O'Ballivan to Tanner Quinn's farm, but it's the rancher's love that might cause her to stay.

A STONE CREEK CHRISTMAS
Available December 2008
from Silhouette Special Edition

Tanner heard the rig roll in around sunset. Smiling, he wandered to the window. Watched as Olivia O'Ballivan climbed out of her Suburban, flung one defiant glance toward the house and started for the barn, the golden retriever trotting along behind her.

Taking his coat and hat down from the peg next to the back door, he put them on and went outside. He was used to being alone, even liked it, but keeping company with Doc O'Ballivan, bristly though she sometimes was, would provide a welcome diversion.

He gave her time to reach the horse Butterpie's stall, then walked into the barn.

The golden retriever came to greet him, all wagging tail and melting brown eyes, and he bent to stroke her soft, sturdy back. "Hey, there, dog," he said.

Sure enough, Olivia was in the stall, brushing Butterpie down and talking to her in a soft, soothing voice that touched something private inside Tanner and made him want to turn on one heel and beat it back to the house.

He'd be damned if he'd do it, though.

This was *his* ranch, *his* barn. Well-intentioned as she was, *Olivia* was the trespasser here, not him.

"She's still very upset," Olivia told him, without turning to look at him or slowing down with the brush.

Shiloh, always an easy horse to get along with, stood contentedly in his own stall, munching away on the feed Tanner had given him earlier. Butterpie, he noted, hadn't touched her supper as far as he could tell.

"Do you know anything at all about horses, Mr. Quinn?" Olivia asked.

He leaned against the stall door, the way he had the day before, and grinned. He'd practically been raised on horseback; he and Tessa had grown up on their grandmother's farm in the Texas hill country, after their folks divorced and went their separate ways, both of them too busy to bother with a couple of kids. "A few things," he said. "And I mean to call you Olivia, so you might as well return the favor and address me by my first name."

He watched as she took that in, dealt with it, decided on an approach. He'd have to wait and see what that turned out to be, but he didn't mind. It was a pleasure just watching Olivia O'Ballivan grooming a horse.

"All right, *Tanner,*" she said. "This barn is a disgrace. When are you going to have the roof fixed? If it snows again, the hay will get wet and probably mold..."

He chuckled, shifted a little. He'd have a crew out there the following Monday morning to replace the roof and shore up the walls—he'd made the arrangements over a week before—but he felt no particular compunction to explain that. He was enjoying her ire too much; it made her color rise and her hair fly when she turned her head, and the faster breathing made her perfect breasts go up and down in an enticing rhythm. "What makes you so sure I'm a greenhorn?" he asked mildly, still leaning on the gate.

At last she looked straight at him, but she didn't move from

Butterpie's side. "Your hat, your boots—that fancy red truck you drive. I'll bet it's customized."

Tanner grinned. Adjusted his hat. "Are you telling me real cowboys don't drive red trucks?"

"There are lots of trucks around here," she said. "Some of them are red, and some of them are new. And *all* of them are splattered with mud or manure or both."

"Maybe I ought to put in a car wash, then," he teased. "Sounds like there's a market for one. Might be a good investment."

She softened, though not significantly, and spared him a cautious half smile, full of questions she probably wouldn't ask. "There's a good car wash in Indian Rock," she informed him. "People go there. It's only forty miles."

"Oh," he said with just a hint of mockery. "*Only* forty miles. Well, then. Guess I'd better dirty up my truck if I want to be taken seriously in these here parts. Scuff up my boots a bit, too, and maybe stomp on my hat a couple of times."

Her cheeks went a fetching shade of pink. "You are twisting what I said," she told him, brushing Butterpie again, her touch gentle but sure. "I meant…"

Tanner envied that little horse. Wished he had a furry hide, so he'd need brushing, too.

"You *meant* that I'm not a real cowboy," he said. "And you could be right. I've spent a lot of time on construction sites over the last few years, or in meetings where a hat and boots wouldn't be appropriate. Instead of digging out my old gear, once I decided to take this job, I just bought new."

"I bet you don't even *have* any old gear," she challenged, but she was smiling, albeit cautiously, as though she might withdraw into a disapproving frown at any second.

He took off his hat, extended it to her. "Here," he teased. "Rub that around in the muck until it suits you."

She laughed, and the sound—well, it caused a powerful and wholly unexpected shift inside him. Scared the hell out of him and, paradoxically, made him yearn to hear it again.

* * * * *

Discover how this rugged rancher's wanderlust is tamed
in time for a merry Christmas, in
A STONE CREEK CHRISTMAS.
In stores December 2008.

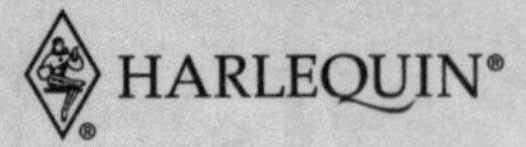
HARLEQUIN®

Coming Next Month

Season's greetings from Harlequin Romance®! Festive miracles, mistletoe kisses and winter weddings to get you into the holiday spirit as we bring you Christmas treats aplenty this month....

#4063 CINDERELLA AND THE COWBOY Judy Christenberry
With her two young children in tow, struggling widow Elizabeth stepped onto the Ransom Homestead looking for the family she'd never had. Despite being welcomed with open arms by the children's grandfather, it's blue-eyed rancher Jack who Elizabeth dreams will make their family complete....

#4064 THE ITALIAN'S MIRACLE FAMILY Lucy Gordon
Heart to Heart
Betrayed by their cheating partners, Alysa and Drago strike an unlikely friendship. But Alysa's calm facade hides a painful secret, which twists every time she sees Drago's child. Can the healing miracle of love make them a family?

#4065 HIS MISTLETOE BRIDE Cara Colter
Police officer Brody hates Christmas. Then vivacious Lila arrives in Snow Mountain and tilts his world sideways. But there's a glimmer of sadness in her soulful eyes. Until, snowbound in a log cabin, Brody claims a kiss under the mistletoe....

#4066 HER BABY'S FIRST CHRISTMAS Susan Meier
When millionaire Jared rescues Elise and her cute baby, Molly, and drives them home for the holidays, he finds himself reluctantly drawn to the tiny family. Elise secretly hopes that gorgeous Jared will stay for Molly's first Christmas—and forever!

#4067 MARRY-ME CHRISTMAS Shirley Jump
A Bride for All Seasons
A ruthless and successful journalist, Flynn never mixes business with pleasure. But when he's sent to write a scathing review of Samantha's bakery, her beauty and innocence catches him off guard. Has this small-town girl unlocked the city-slicker's heart?

#4068 PREGNANT: FATHER WANTED Claire Baxter
Baby on Board
There is more to Italian playboy Ric than he lets the world see. And pregnant travel writer Lyssa is determined to find out what. She's fiercely independent, but could Ric, in fact, be the perfect husband and father for her baby?

HRCNM1108